W9-BZC-800

"You'll have to excuse the mess."

Adam spoke to her over one wide shoulder as he crossed the room. "The girls didn't pick up their toys."

"I like a little disorder." Cheyenne wasn't fooled by his tone. She looked around at the comfortable furniture and caught a glimpse of a tidy kitchen. Not only did he work hard as a doctor, he had made a home for his daughters.

As she remembered how her father had done the same, her throat caught with emotion. Dad had put in long days in the barns and on the range, but he was always there to listen to stories of the school day, help with homework, praise good grades and sympathize with childhood heartaches. As she crossed the room, she saw the same commitment in this home. Hard not to respect and admire Adam for the man he was, a man who did whatever was required to take care of those he loved.

Her feelings for him had changed. She didn't want to admit it, but they had.

Books by Jillian Hart

Love Inspired

*A Soldier for Christmas
*Precious Blessings
*Every Kind of Heaven
*Everyday Blessings
*A McKaslin Homecoming
A Holiday to Remember
*Her Wedding Wish
*Her Perfect Man
Homefront Holiday
*A Soldier for Keeps
*Blind-Date Bride
†The Soldier's Holiday Vow
†The Rancher's Promise
Klondike Hero
†His Holiday Bride
†His Country Girl
†Wyoming Sweethearts
Mail-Order Christmas Brides
  "Her Christmas Family"
†Hometown Hearts

Love Inspired Historical

*Homespun Bride
*High Country Bride
In a Mother's Arms
  "Finally a Family"
**Gingham Bride
**Patchwork Bride
**Calico Bride
**Snowflake Bride

*The McKaslin Clan
†The Granger Family Ranch
**Buttons & Bobbins

JILLIAN HART

grew up on her family's homestead, where she helped raise cattle, rode horses and scribbled stories in her spare time. After earning her English degree from Whitman College, she worked in travel and advertising before selling her first novel. When Jillian isn't working on her next story, she can be found puttering in her rose garden, curled up with a good book or spending quiet evenings at home with her family.

Hometown Hearts
Jillian Hart

Love Inspired

If you purchased this book without a cover you should be aware that this book is stolen property. It was reported as "unsold and destroyed" to the publisher, and neither the author nor the publisher has received any payment for this "stripped book."

Recycling programs
for this product may
not exist in your area.

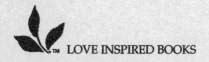

LOVE INSPIRED BOOKS

ISBN-13: 978-0-373-81600-2

HOMETOWN HEARTS

Copyright © 2012 by Jill Strickler

All rights reserved. Except for use in any review, the reproduction or utilization of this work in whole or in part in any form by any electronic, mechanical or other means, now known or hereafter invented, including xerography, photocopying and recording, or in any information storage or retrieval system, is forbidden without the written permission of the editorial office, Love Inspired Books, 233 Broadway, New York, NY 10279 U.S.A.

This is a work of fiction. Names, characters, places and incidents are either the product of the author's imagination or are used fictitiously, and any resemblance to actual persons, living or dead, business establishments, events or locales is entirely coincidental.

This edition published by arrangement with Love Inspired Books.

® and TM are trademarks of Love Inspired Books, used under license. Trademarks indicated with ® are registered in the United States Patent and Trademark Office, the Canadian Trade Marks Office and in other countries.

www.LoveInspiredBooks.com

Printed in U.S.A.

Your word is a lamp to my feet
and a light to my path.
—*Psalms* 119:105

Chapter One

"Good boy, Toby." Dr. Cheyenne Granger laughed as the hound dog standing on her examining table swiped her chin with his tongue. She may have been just out of vet school but she was so happy with her choice of profession she could not contain her joy. She wrapped her arms around the elderly canine.

"You are such a good patient." She lowered him gently to the floor and gave his ears a rub. "Are we friends again?"

Big chocolate eyes forgave her for having stuck him with a needle a few moments before.

"Thanks, buddy." No one on earth could forgive the way a dog could. "Are you ready to find your mom?"

Toby swiped her face a second time and wagged his tail. "Yes! Let's go!" he seemed to say as he tilted his head to one side and glanced toward the closed door.

"Then lead the way, handsome." She seized his leash. Toby knew the path down the short hallway past the patient rooms to the waiting area where the air-conditioning blew against the hot summer Wyoming sunshine. Several dogs panted with nervousness alongside their owners, waiting for their appointments. One particularly unhappy cat yowled from a carrier in the corner.

"Toby!" Terri Baker Gold rose from one of the cushy chairs and hurried over. The dog gave a cry of relief and raced into his owner's arms. "What a good boy. Did you think I wouldn't be waiting for you? I would never leave you, baby."

The hound licked Terri's chin at the reassurance. Happy that his appointment was over, he wagged his tail and looked expectantly at the door.

"We should get the results from the lab in a few days. I'll give you a call. Other than that, I've sent a prescription over to the pharmacy." Cheyenne grabbed a biscuit from the bowl on the counter and held the bone-shaped treat out to Toby. "You let Terri know if you don't feel better, okay, boy?"

The old dog took the treat politely, crunching away with canine satisfaction on his face.

"Thanks, Cheyenne." Terri, a lifelong friend, smiled. "Nate must be thrilled to have you join his practice."

"He hasn't tossed me out yet," she quipped from behind the counter where the receptionist, Tasha Wisener, chatted on the phone. Multiple lines were lit up; another busy day. "I'm the one who is thrilled to be here. I'm grateful Nate has taken me under his wing. I wouldn't want to work anywhere else."

"Especially with so much going on in your family." Terri opened her purse and pulled out her checkbook. "The Grangers have had two weddings already with two more to come. Then there's Rori's pregnancy and rumors about Frank and Cady."

"Yes, and you're about the hundredth person who has hinted for insider information on Dad's intentions toward a certain inn owner." She couldn't help laughing. Her dad's quiet romance with Cady Winslow had become the talk of the town. "I'm the last to know anything. Besides, even if I did know something and admitted it, guess what would happen next?"

"Me. I would happen," Tasha intervened. She hung up the phone and tapped a few computer keys. Terri's bill popped out of the printer. "I would repeat it, my mother-in-law would get wind of it and the whole county would know by nightfall. Nothing is private in a small town."

"And if it is, not for long." Cheyenne grabbed the next patient's chart—the Stone family, who didn't yet have a pet of their own but had been to the clinic twice already. Little Julianna had a rescuer's heart.

Wondering what had brought the Stone sisters in today, Cheyenne straightened her white coat, opened the door and walked into the cozy examining room. Sunlight streamed through the window and tumbled onto the soft, buttery walls and tile floor. Two chairs flanked the window, one filled by a tween wearing a frown, a fashionable summery top, shorts and matching sandals. The other girl, grade school–aged Julianna, clutched a shoe box. Tiny holes had been punctured in the lid to let in air.

"Cheyenne!" Her brown pigtails bobbed as she held out the box. "It's a baby bird. A hawk caught him and I waved the yard rake at him until he let the baby go."

"Sorry," Jenny apologized with a big-sister-in-charge attitude. "I told her not to bother. But she insisted. I don't think there's anything you can do."

"I can't let her suffer." Julianna blinked back tears and her button face crinkled with the pain she felt for the bird. "It says in the Bible that God loves the sparrows. This is a finch, but I'm sure He loves finches, too."

"I know He does." Cheyenne took the box gently, worried over what she would find inside. "I'll take a look and see what we can do to help this little guy."

"She's a girl, or I hope she is. I named her Tomasina. Everybody needs a name." Julianna sniffled, doing her best to be brave and hold back her tears of concern. Her sister fought the same concern by lifting her chin as if she *so* did not care.

Cheyenne wasn't fooled. This was the sisters' third visit since she'd joined Dr. Cannon's practice. She understood what the girls could not say. She carefully placed the shoe box on the metal examining table and eased off the lid.

Tucked in the corner and huddled in a cozy bed made of a soft hand towel—a brand-new guest towel by the looks of it—lay a baby goldfinch, tiny and fragile. Broken bits of down littered the towel. The creature trembled, terrified and in pain.

Julianna squeezed her eyes shut, her fingers steepling in prayer. Cheyenne could feel the force of it from where she stood, a child's pure, unselfish wish. Surely the good Lord would hear such an honorable request.

"Hey, Tomasina." She spoke softly, willing all the calmness she could into her voice. "It's good to meet you. I imagine you are really missing your mama."

The baby bird tilted its head to focus on her. The little heart beat wildly, tapping against the fluffy down on its breast. How terrifying this had to be and how alone the chick must feel.

"You are safe, little one." The finch was too young to fly and probably too paralyzed with fear to move. Tenderly, she scooped the tiny bundle into the palm of her hand and held it carefully so the bird felt secure. Sure enough, talon marks tracked around the exposed abdomen, puncturing the skin where claws had dug in. They didn't look too deep, but with such a tiny creature they didn't have to be.

"See, right here?" She took the time to hold the finch for Julianna's inspection. The girl came closer, eyes wide and bottom lip trembling when she saw the contusions. "That's where she's bleeding. I need to clean the wounds and tend them."

"She's not going to d-die?"

"I don't know, but I promise to take good care of her."

"I know you will." Julianna gently stroked

the bird's soft head with the tip of her forefinger. "You've got to be all right, Tomasina. Be sure and do what Dr. Granger says."

The little girl was too cute. Cheyenne bit her lip. The bird in her hands relaxed a bit. Maybe the creature realized she was not in any danger or perhaps her fear was too overwhelming. She needed to get the little one into the back and cared for. "If you girls want to go home, I'll call you and let you know how she's doing."

"Will it be very long?" Julianna took charge of the abandoned shoe box and lid. "Can we stay?"

Hard to look into those big brown eyes and say no. "Go ahead and hang out in the waiting room but give your dad a call. He needs to know where you are. This could take a while."

"Oh! *Dad.*" An "uh-oh" look puckered her adorable face. Julianna seemed to expect her father might not be pleased with this latest development.

Probably the dad feared he was about to be surprised with a vet bill. Well, she would waive the charges, just as she had before. The last thing she wanted was to make Julianna think she shouldn't step up and help God's creatures. She opened the door. While she hadn't officially met Dr. Stone yet, she'd heard good things about him. She had spotted him enough times around town, at Cady's inn and her sister's wedding to have gathered an impression about the man.

Serious. Subdued. Not exactly social. Striking, broad shoulders…wait, where had *that* come from?

She saw the girls off in the direction of the waiting room before heading into the back with the bird huddled in her palm.

"The Stone kids again?" Ivy Tipple, their tech, looked up from checking on the black Lab in one of the kennels recovering from his emergency surgery, the blood pressure cuff in hand.

"How did you know?"

"Who else would bring in a baby bird, considering this economy and the cost of a vet bill? Do you need a hand?"

"No, go ahead and finish with Buster. He's looking much better." The Lab's tongue still lolled but his eyes were open.

"He's doing well. He's going to survive his fight with that coyote. Way to go, Buster." Ivy knelt to her work, catching the swish and pulse of the Lab's heart with the Doppler. The sound filled the back room, and Cheyenne gave thanks for the steady beat. The Lab had a close call.

"His blood pressure is not only up, it's perfect," Ivy announced. "You did good today, too, Doc."

"Just doin' my job." The one God had blessed her with. She opened the nearby cabinet with her free hand, sorting through the supplies she would need, praying she could make a difference for the little creature in her palm. She couldn't disappoint Julianna Stone with her big, soulful brown eyes.

"It's a personal call, Doctor."

Adam Stone didn't need to ask who it was from. He knew only three people in this small town well enough to be called personal—two of whom were his daughters. He wasn't interested in making friends during his temporary stay. No, this extended visit to Wyoming was not permanent. He did not anticipate getting attached to anyone in this tiny rural town. "Have them hold. I'll be right there, Mildred."

"All right." The matronly woman closed the door to the exam room, leaving him alone with his patient.

"Sorry about that," he apologized, although the elderly lady seated on the table didn't seem to mind the intrusion.

"Oh, I know what it's like to have young children." Mrs. Tipple's face was wreathed with lovely good humor. "Mine were a handful. I don't know how working women do it these days. I couldn't keep up with my brood and that's all I had to do. I think I'm still worn-out from it."

A sweet lady. "Your daughter was in last week. She's fifty-five, so it's been a while since she was twelve."

"Yes, but it seems like yesterday. You just wait. Time flies. There's no stopping it." Mrs. Tipple's eyes twinkled. "So, how's my ticker?"

"Your heart is stable for now. I'll call in your medication renewal." He offered the lady his hand to help her down. "You're still using the pharmacy in town?"

"For the last sixty years."

Hard to beat that. He'd learned that Wild Horse, Wyoming, was about as stable as life could get. He opened the door for his charming patient. "You call me if you have any concerns."

"Yes, Doctor. You have a nice day, now."

"You, too, Mrs. Tipple." He waited while the elderly lady tapped out of the doorway on her sensible heels before he headed to his office at the end of the hall. One of the lines was flashing and he grabbed the receiver. "What is it this time?"

"Dad?" There was noise in the background

making it hard to hear his youngest daughter. "Are you in a good mood?"

"Not really." Julianna's question was always a sign that he wasn't going to like whatever she had to say. He dropped into his chair. "What have you done now?"

Before she could answer, he dug out an aspirin bottle from his top desk drawer. He figured he might need it, as single parenting was harder than it looked. A strange yowling carried across the line, interrupted by a dog's ringing bark.

"Daddy, don't get mad." Hard not to recognize her guilty tone. "I *had* to help her."

"Help who?"

"Tomasina."

Tomasina? He racked his brain for any information associated with that name. No children, no neighbors, no neighborhood pets that he could think of. He pried the lid off the bottle. "Time to explain, young lady."

"She could be dying, Daddy." Julianna sniffled. Her feelings were so tender and drove up the high notes in her voice. "I had to bring her here."

The picture came clear. A dog barked in the background again, harmonized by an cat's howl and a woman's voice telling Grover to sit like a good boy. No mystery where the girl was.

"Haven't I told you not to go across town to the vet's office without clearing it with me?" He shook out two aspirin and popped them into his mouth, not even bothering with water.

"Y-yes." Julianna's tone went to a near whisper. His guess, she was kneeling on the floor, holding herself in, contrite and wounded. She'd been fragile since the divorce. "Daddy, are you mad?"

"Very." He didn't know how to begin to explain it all. "Tell me about Tomasina."

"I couldn't let her get gobbled up." Misery quivered in her voice. "She was bleeding, so I held her while Jenny made up a shoe box like a nest and we hurried to the vet, except we had to walk careful so we wouldn't shake Tomasina."

Still no idea who or what Tomasina was, but it didn't matter. His daughter felt it was her duty to save everything and everyone. He was at a loss how to make her understand. She couldn't save the world. Why wasn't she like other kids, busy playing with their toys, wanting the latest video game and trying to listen to unacceptable music on their MP3 players?

She was too much like the boy he'd once been, thinking God cared for every creature great and small.

"Dr. Stone?" Mildred tapped on his open

door. "Your four o'clock canceled. Just thought you should know."

"Thanks. Why don't we call it a day?"

Mildred nodded, bustling off to close up shop and forward the calls to his cell because there was no answering service to hire in this town.

"Stay right where you are, Julianna." He rubbed at his right temple. The pain in his skull drilled like a jackhammer. "I'll be over in five minutes."

"Am I gr-ounded?"

He winced at how little and young she sounded. He shrugged off his white coat. "We'll see. Is Jenny with you?"

"Yes, but don't punish her. Please? It's not her fault. I *made* her come with me."

That was Julianna, caring about everyone ahead of herself.

"I'll take that into consideration." He pushed out of the chair, hung his coat over the back of it and grabbed his keys off his desk. "I'm on my way."

"O-kay." She gulped audibly, fearing her punishment to come.

Grounding her was not working. He hung up the phone and marched to the door, remembering his patient. Mrs. Tipple had said her children had been a full-time job in and of themselves. He wished he had that kind of time to give to them. He'd wanted to hire a babysitter but Jenny had raised an earsplitting argument, pointing out that she was old enough to *be* a babysitter so she did not need one.

Life was changing and it was getting more complicated. But the girls were prospering here, where the pain of their mother's abandonment wasn't a constant reminder. That was the reason he'd locked up his town house, put his practice on hold and moved to Wyoming for the rest of the summer.

All this change, as temporary as it was, was tough on him. He called a goodbye to Mildred and pushed out the back door of the practice the town doctor had asked him to join. He breathed in the scent of freshly mown grass on the warm breeze and felt calmer. Overhead, leaves whispered from the old maples marching on both sides of the narrow street.

"Howdy, Doc!" Chip Baker shouted over the sound of his lawn mower and touched the brim of his cowboy hat.

"Hi." He beeped the remote to his BMW.

"Your girls wandered by here a little bit ago," Chip called out, always a friendly sort. "They looked in a real hurry. Something about a sick bird."

The mystery of Tomasina solved. Someone

from the house next door came out to complain to Chip about the noise, so Adam slid into his car, started the engine and was more than happy to drive away from the scene.

Dappled shade tumbled over him as he headed down the street. Folks sat on front porches sipping tea. He spotted more than half a dozen women out working in their flower beds as he drove past and two people waved him to a stop on his way to Main Street to tell him about his daughters.

People were definitely friendly here, and it made him uncomfortable. He wasn't unfriendly as much as private, and the fact that everyone knew what his girls were up to besides him didn't sit well. What kind of father was he? He pulled into one of the parking spots in the vet clinic lot, his head still pounding. Frustrated, he tossed his sunglasses on the console and felt a brush against the side of his face, something as soft and rare as an angel's wing.

He looked up, inexorably drawn to the front window. There in the lobby speaking with his daughters was the loveliest woman with red-brown hair, big blue eyes and a sweetheart's face. Amazingly lovely. She made the world disappear when she smiled at his girls.

The infamous Dr. Granger. The *gorgeous* Dr. Granger. He watched as she smoothed a lock of flyaway hair out of Julianna's eyes. The woman wasn't only stunning, but kind. His palms broke into a sweat just like last time he'd spotted her from afar. His heart skipped a beat. He forgot to breathe. He felt a little unsteady.

She moved out of sight, bending down as if to kneel before his daughters and became lost in the glare of the sun on the glass. Although she vanished from his view, his heart smarted as if stung.

It wasn't a good sign. Not good, at all.

Chapter Two

Somehow his feet carried him to the door as if he were in a daze. Maybe it was the heat wave sucking the moisture from his body and dehydrating his brain. That had to be it. His sweaty palms gripped the door handle with a slight slide. Embarrassing. Maybe he could attribute that to dehydration, too.

"Uh-oh. Dad's here."

He recognized the dour tone in his oldest's voice. She was, after all, practicing to be a teenager.

Air-conditioning breezed over him as he released hold of the door. It swooshed shut behind him and an angry yowling protest rose from a cat carrier on the floor nearby. A dog bounced up from his sprawl on the floor to bark a ringing welcome while a frizzy-haired woman tried to gently shush him, to no avail.

His gaze shot to Cheyenne against his will like an arrow to a target.

He'd never seen her up close. Even more striking. She had a sloping nose, a wide smile that would make movie actresses envious. With her high cheekbones, golden sunny complexion and a willowy grace, she made a breathtaking picture as she rose from kneeling before Julianna's chair. The vet's white jacket might make her look professional, but she glowed with a cheerful joy that had a beauty all its own.

He wasn't captivated, really. He could look away if he wanted to, except his eyes didn't seem to be cooperating.

"Daddy!" Julianna bopped to her feet, bounded across the tile and wrapped her arms around his waist. The four dogs in the waiting room barked in excitement, eager to join in. The cacophony was deafening. His daughter's big brown eyes peered up at him, fringed by long dark lashes and her thick, flyaway bangs. "Please don't be mad anymore. I'll stay in my room every evening after supper with no toys. I p-promise."

His heart caved. "I don't see the use in sending you to your room if it doesn't change your behavior." He tweaked her nose, at a loss what to do with the girl. "I'll have to think of something more effective."

"I could give up desserts?"

Hard to stay mad at that little face. He steeled his resolve, trying not to be too lenient and also not to give in to his anger from the worry she'd caused him.

"She shouldn't be deciding her own punishment, Dad." Jenny sauntered up. Her dark eyes hadn't lost the look of pain and anger at her mother, but the stay in Wyoming had helped to ease it. She gave an I-so-don't-care scowl and flipped a lock of her hair. "*I* don't get to decide my punishments."

"I'll think of something fair." It was all he could promise. His neurotransmitters weren't firing correctly because of the woman walking toward him. She had the power to suck the oxygen from the atmosphere and all rational thought from his brain. It only got worse with each step she took closer.

He couldn't tear his attention away from her. He noticed things about her he'd tried not to see before. Her hair was lighter than he'd thought, full of russets and golds and strawberry-blond shades as it fell in soft tendrils from her French braid. Gently swooping bangs framed the bluest eyes he'd ever seen. From a distance, she'd been beautiful. Up close, she was stunning in a gentle, natural girl-next-door way.

"Dr. Stone." She plunged her hands into her

jacket pockets and offered him a professional smile. "At last we meet."

"There was no way to avoid it." He heard his voice boom low as if with dislike and internally he winced. He wasn't proud of the tone. After his divorce, he had put up so many walls, and he didn't like that about himself. He automatically wanted women to keep their distance so he wouldn't be duped like that again.

She didn't seem to know what to say. She opened her mouth, hesitated, bit her bottom lip for a moment. "It's a pleasure to meet you. You have the most wonderful girls."

"You don't know them like I do." Those words had sounded lighter in his head, but on his voice they seemed to weigh down like iron. Unlikable, remote, unfeeling iron.

"Daddy, Tomasina's better." Julianna bounced away to hold out her hand to one of the nearby dogs. "Cheyenne says she has a good chance. If she lives, we can put her back in her nest."

"Her mother won't take her now," he blurted out, realizing too late what he'd said. He prayed his comment wouldn't remind the girls of what they'd lost. A mother who had only part-time interest in them.

"Actually, that's not true." Cheyenne Granger looked all too happy to correct him. "Julianna knows where the nest is, so we should be able to return the baby to her home. Once Tomasina is back with her siblings, she should be just fine. They are probably looking around the nest wondering where she is."

"Or saying she shouldn't have misbehaved, which made her fall out of the nest in the first place," Jenny supplied with a faint grin. "I have a lot of experience with siblings."

He ruffled Jenny's hair. "That's a relief. Under no circumstances are we keeping a bird in the house."

"It wouldn't be right to keep her locked up," Julianna informed him. "God meant for her to fly in the sky. She would be sad in a cage."

"That's right." Cheyenne's gentleness drew his attention.

There was something luminous about her and he had noticed it before. When he'd seen her last, she had been wearing a bridesmaid's dress at the family wedding he'd attended a while ago. He couldn't forget the way she'd stood out to him above all the other women in the room. He was not so good with words, which had been one of Stacy's greatest complaints about him. His lack of words became a problem again as silence settled in, but the beautiful veterinarian didn't seem bothered by it. She knelt to catch Julianna's chin with both of her slender, gentle hands, a show of affection that surprised him.

"You keep right on helping animals. You call me anytime, got it?" She was at ease with his daughters, sharing a smile with Julianna and then with Jenny.

"Okay, I will. Animals just find me."

"More like you find them," Jenny corrected and shared an understanding smile with Cheyenne. He appreciated her kindness to his girls.

"Adam, this visit is entirely on me. You won't be billed." She opened and held the door for them. "Julianna and Jenny did a great job of rescuing Tomasina and getting her here safely. They saved her life. You must be proud of them."

"I suppose I'll keep them. For now." He caught each girl with one arm and drew them outside into the sun and heat. He should thank the lady for her help and her gentleness to his daughters, but he wasn't sure how that would sound. Too grateful, too familiar—would it open himself up too much?

Silence settled between them. He couldn't ignore the wall he put up between himself and women. It was a gut reaction he didn't know how to stop.

"Saving lives must run in the family." Cheyenne raised a hand to shield her eyes.

"I don't save anyone." The words came out harsher than he meant them. Again.

"What do you mean? You saved little Owen's life. Last winter you didn't have to get involved when he was having problems breathing at the diner. You could have gone about your dinner, minding your own business, but you got involved. Since Owen is about to become my nephew at the end of the month, my family thinks mighty highly of you."

"That's because they don't know me. Give them time and they will change their minds." The girls broke away from him to scamper off to the car.

"You're mighty humble for a big-city doctor." Cheyenne squinted up at him.

"I'm not so big or humble. I do what I can, just the way you do. Life matters. That's why I work hard at what I do."

"Me, too." Their gazes met and locked. Finally, she'd gotten an almost smile out of him. Adam Stone towered above her at an impressive height; he had to be about the same six foot three as her dad.

Handsome would describe him, but *remarkable* would be a better word. His granite face was a tad too rugged to be classically handsome, but he could outshine George Clooney and all the doctors on any medical show she'd ever watched. He wore all black from his tie to his dress shoes. Since Wild Horse was a casual place, Adam Stone was as out of water as a fish could get. He didn't look like a kindred spirit, yet they had this in common. They both valued life; they both fought for it.

"I like making a difference and knowing I can ease suffering." She walked with him to his door, squinting in the sunshine. "Is that why you decided to become a doctor, too?"

"I'm in it strictly for the money." The promise of a smile dug into the corners of his mouth, dazzling enough to light up his deep brown eyes. "That's why I came out here for the rest of the summer. Manhattan wasn't lucrative enough."

"Yes, and I can see Wild Horse is." She had patients waiting, but did her feet take her back down the walkway? No. They remained stuck to the concrete, immovable. "Your workday must be a lot more leisurely here."

"I had three appointments all day, which gives me plenty of time to get to know my new patients. It's a change of pace."

"I already know my patients before they walk in the door."

"You are one of those animal people, aren't you? You can't walk past a furry creature without stopping to get acquainted."

"You have no idea." The man radiated the emotion of a mountain—solemn, somber, closed off—except for his dark eyes. Sadness lived in them, veiled and shadowed but there all the same. She didn't know why she could read all of that. "I've been this way for as long as anyone can remember. Dad tells stories of me helping him doctor the cattle when I was barely old enough to talk."

"Medicine was all I ever wanted to do, too." He stared at the keys in hand and shrugged wide, dependable shoulders. "Best get the girls home. Thanks for, uh, saving Tomasina."

"Anytime." She jammed her hands into her white jacket, feeling oddly sad for the man. Everyone heard how his wife had left him and his daughters for his best friend, a fellow doctor who shared his former practice. How hard that had to have been for him, she sympathized, remembering how shattered her father had been years ago when her mother had left him for another man. Adam Stone didn't look shattered. He seemed invincible, as if no tragedy could ever touch him.

She wanted to say something of comfort or reassurance, but she didn't know what would possibly be appropriate. They were strangers. She knew his daughters but not the man, who managed a craggy half smile in lieu of a goodbye.

"This isn't over yet." She backed away, waving through the sun-streaked windshield to the girls buckled up inside the sedan. "You are invited to our family's Fourth of July bash tomorrow."

"Apparently there's no getting out of it." His wry tone held the hint of a smile although his face betrayed no emotion. He angled behind the wheel and shut the door.

That was it. No goodbye. No looking-forward-to-seeing-you-again comments. Just the hum of a finely tuned engine rolling over. She watched the luxury car sail away, the vehicle at odds with the practical pickups and four-wheel drives in the lot, out of place just like the man.

She headed back inside where her next furry patient awaited her, but she couldn't get Adam Stone out of her mind.

"You're a little late for supper, girl."

She looked up at her dad's comment, her feet dragging on the pathway from the garage to the backyard. An old maple spread broad-leafed shade over the picnic table set up on the lawn, where her family was eating. Signs of preparation for tomorrow's bash were already up. Strings of lights hung from the porch eaves and stretched to wind around the maple's lowest branches. A fire pit had been dug in the gravel at the edge of the lawn, stacked with wood and ready to burn.

"Long day." Exhausted, she dropped her bag on the lawn. "Three emergencies, a packed schedule and a couple drop-ins that I worked in after hours and a rescued baby finch."

"Tomasina?" Cady Winslow grabbed the iced tea pitcher and filled a plastic cup.

"So you heard." Cheyenne dropped onto the seat beside her sister Addison and reached across the table to accept the iced tea Cady offered.

"Even I know who Tomasina is," Dad quipped as he popped a barbecued potato chip into his mouth. "Julianna told me all about it when I picked Cady up just a bit ago."

"Poor Tomasina," Addy sympathized as she poked at her hot dog, adjusting the bun. "Is she going to make a full recovery?"

"She was doing much better when I left. Ivy volunteered to take her home. So far her prognosis is good." She lifted the paper plate serving as a lid over her meal. The smoky scent of barbecued hot dog made her stomach rumble. The generous scoops of their housekeeper's potato salad made her mouth water. "Mrs. Gunderson spoils us. I hope she never leaves."

"I just gave her a raise to make sure of it." Dad chuckled as he polished off the last of the potato salad on his plate. "I'm going in for seconds. Anyone want more?"

"I do." Cady's gentle green eyes softened when she focused on Dad. Honest love made her even more radiant. She rose from the bench with grace, taking her plate with her. The sun shone in the soft waves of her pretty brown hair and her sandals didn't seem to touch the ground as she crossed the grass.

The way Dad watched the woman's approach made Cheyenne's vision blur. She loved that her dad had found someone to treasure him the way he deserved. It was sweet when he drew Cady toward him and they walked the rest of the distance together. The couple's happiness lifted on the temperate breeze like the low, merry murmurings of their conversation.

"I'm glad Dad found Cady." Addy sighed a little, too. "I've never seen him this happy."

"No, neither have I. She's good for him."

"They are good for each other."

They sat in silence, watching the middle-aged couple cross the porch, their quiet laughter carrying on the breeze. Dad held the screen door for his lady love.

"When do you think he is going to propose?"

Addy tossed a lock of strawberry-blond hair over her shoulder, her big blue eyes full of mischief.

"How should I know? Like Dad tells me anything more than he tells you." She clasped her hands together, wanting to say the blessing before her stomach imploded with hunger. She'd missed lunch.

"I think it will be soon. Just a guess. No, more like a wild hope." Addy crunched on a potato chip. "I think Cady will make a good stepmom, don't you?"

"The best." She tried to close her eyes for the blessing, but her gaze zipped across the lawn to the house. Large picture windows looked in at the family room and gave a sliver of a view into the kitchen where Dad stole Cady's plate, set it on the breakfast bar and pulled her into his arms. Tenderness radiated from their embrace. As their lips met, Addy sighed again.

"I don't think Dad knows we can see him." Cheyenne watched with interest. "We shouldn't be spying."

"If he doesn't want us to spy on him, next time he should close the blinds." Addy's grin stretched from ear to ear, showing off the dimples she'd inherited from their father. "I think he's getting serious."

"I do, too." She tried to look away, but the way her dad ended the kiss with reverence and tugged Cady against his chest, as if he cherished her above all else, made it impossible. Her father had never dated once in the seventeen years since their mother left. His heart had never recovered from the betrayal and his life had been too busy with the responsibility of raising five kids and running one of the largest ranches in White Horse County. He'd been lonely for so long.

Father, thank You for sending someone to love Dad. Thank You for sending Cady. She bowed her head, finishing the prayer with thanks for the blessings in her life, so very many blessings. She opened her eyes. Dad and Cady had stepped out of sight but the feel of their happiness remained.

"So, do you have tomorrow off for sure or not?" Addy chose another chip from the pile on her plate.

Before she could answer, a cow leaned across the wooden rails of the fence at the far edge of the lawn, pleaded with doelike eyes and gave a long, sorrowful moo.

"No chips for you, Buttercup, sorry." Cheyenne grabbed the plastic bottle of relish and squirted it the length of her hot dog bun. "Addy, tomorrow I'm on call."

"Bummer. You're always on call."

"That's because there are two vets in a fifty-mile radius." She traded the relish for the mayonnaise bottle and gave it a squeeze. "Nate is going to take the big animal calls, if there are any. I'm taking the small animal."

"You look happy, too." Addy licked barbecue seasoning off her fingertips. "It's good to see. You must be over your broken heart."

"Over it? I don't even remember it." That was what denial could do for a girl. She was the queen of denial. She could block out nearly any hurt, any heartache, any disappointment. In fact, she couldn't even remember what had happened with what's-his-name back in vet school. Broken heart? Her heart was just fine as long as she didn't have to look at it. "I'm my own independent woman. What's there not to be happy about?"

"That's my view, too. Marriage, who needs it?" Addy reached to grab more chips from the bowl in the center of the table. "No man is going to tie me down with matrimony."

"Me, either." Her experience with romance had been enough to make her leery. She thought of how their mom had treated Dad and of every other person she knew who'd been disappointed by love. Her sister-in-law Rori's first marriage hadn't worked out, her soon-to-be sister-in-law Sierra's husband had abandoned her with a small son to raise. She couldn't help recalling Adam Stone's sorrow, a shadow that remained even in full light.

She was a healer and knew some of the worst wounds were not physical. The type she did not know how to treat; she knew of no medicine that would heal them and yet injuries to the heart and spirit happened every day. They left scars in the most vulnerable places, marring the soul.

"Look at Dad." Addy's whisper vibrated with delight. "In front of us, he can barely even hold Cady's hand. Like we couldn't have guessed they were kissing in the kitchen."

"He's bashful," she said because the truth bunched in her throat and she didn't want to say those words and ruin the happy moment as Cady laughed gently. Buttercup let out another moo at not being invited to the picnic table and Dad called out to the cow in his tender, deep-noted baritone.

Dad's wounds still affected him and made it tough for him to bare his vulnerable heart. If she looked past her own denial to how shattered she'd been when Edward broke things off with her, she felt similarly. Love that lasted and stood the test of years and hardship was rare. There was no way to tell ahead of time which relationship would endure and which would fail. That was why she was staying single for a long, long time.

Julianna Howe
relationship would endure and when would
fail. That was always how she, the author of
a long love line.

Chapter Three

"Daddy, why are the cows in the road?"

"I don't know. I'm not a cow expert." Adam stopped in the middle of the country road, since he had no choice. The herd of black cows with snowy faces blocked both lanes. No way around them. He'd always thought cows were flighty and scattered easily but changed his mind as the herd lifted their heads unconcerned at the car's approach. Not one animal shied or ran. On the contrary, the creatures stood their ground like living, breathing tanks.

"They shouldn't be out of their pasture." The click of a seat belt told him his littlest had unbuckled. Julianna poked in between the front seats, straining to see. "I don't recognize any of them."

"How many cows do you know?"

"The Grangers have tons of cows." Julianna

gripped the leather seats and levered herself over the console and into the passenger seat, her gaze riveted on the animals. "I know Buttercup and Jasmine and Daisy and—"

"I get the picture," he interrupted before she could go on and name the "tons" of cows she'd been introduced to one by one. He glanced at the dashboard clock irritably. They were fashionably late, thanks to Jenny who had changed outfits more than half a dozen times before she was fit to be seen in public.

"Can I go say hi?"

"No." He made sure the word boomed with authority. Under no circumstance was his little slip of a daughter walking up to those enormous and dangerous-looking creatures. One animal had horns sticking out of his head. That couldn't be good. Adam hit the car horn in one long blast. Surely honking would startle them into getting out of the way.

Wrong. Instead of bolting, the cows focused on his car with pinpoint accuracy. Dozens upon dozens of brown eyes zeroed in on the newly waxed finish and plodded forward, as if mesmerized by the brightness. They created an impenetrable barrier across the road like soldiers on a march. One bold cow broke out of the pack and lapped the grill with its tongue.

What on earth? Adam hit the horn again,

long and loud. That ought to scare the cow, or at least give it a reason to back off a few feet.

Wrong. Curious, the cow leaned over the hood as if trying to peer into the windshield. The cow seemed as big as a truck and he'd never seen anything in real life with such huge teeth. The mouth opened, that big head shook, a spot of drool splashed on the windshield. At the back of his mind, he remembered the televised images of bulls goring runners on the streets of Spain that had made it to the evening news.

"I wouldn't honk again if I were you, Dad." Jenny crossed her arms, bored in the backseat.

"Yeah, Dad. Do we have anything to eat in the car?" Julianna asked.

The enormous cow's teeth flashed as he bit into the windshield wiper and tugged it away from the glass. It stood up at half-mast, a little crooked. Excited, other cows crowded in, trying to grab it. Tongues tugged at the sideview mirror, others licked at the paint, teeth clamped on the door handles.

Now what did he do? He saw tomorrow's headlines in the little local paper. Sedan Demolished by Bovine Attack.

"Dad, do we have any granola bars?" Julianna giggled as a cow spotted her through the window and tried to lick at her through the glass with swipe after swipe of her big tongue. The car rocked slightly as cows bumped against it.

"You and Jenny ate them. Snacks will spoil your dinner."

"It's not for me." Julianna laughed, the door popped open and the scent of sun-warmed animals and the sound of paint being licked off his new car filled the passenger compartment.

"Young lady, get back in here—" Too late. She was gone, mobbed by the huge creatures who licked at her face, grabbed hold of her pigtails and tugged on her shirt.

"Julianna!" Sheer terror shot through him. He lunged after her, caught short by the tight embrace of the seat belt. Adrenaline pumped through his system but her giggle lifted above the sound of shifting of hooves and his car being mauled.

The cows miraculously looked up and stopped attacking his vehicle. Someone knocked on his driver-side window. A woman with auburn locks and laughing blue eyes appeared through the bovine throng.

Cheyenne Granger.

"Get back, Shrek." She approached the horned behemoth fearlessly and patted him on the nose. "I know it's exciting to be out here on the road, but it's not safe. I hope that windshield wiper isn't bent."

Contrite, the animal offered his nose for a petting.

Adam rolled down his window, hoping the fact that he had trouble breathing didn't show. She affected him, there was no way to deny it. "I wasn't sure what to do. Are the cows safe?"

"They are tame, but as you can see, not harmless if left to their own devices." She shoved the windshield wiper into place. "I'll give the Parnells a call. It looks as if Shrek took down a part of his fence. You like doing that, don't you, buddy?"

The big black-and-white bull—yes, it was really a bull—gave a head toss and focused on the pink phone she'd pulled from her pocket. She was a vet for a reason. Her gentle confidence, her loving laugh as the cows crowded around her trying to grab her cell, the way she lit up with affection as she rubbed noses, scrubbed ears and moved aside for Julianna to join in.

"This is a regular occurrence?" His question drew one cow's attention who came over and stuck her nose through the window. What did he do? "Shoo."

"That's not going to work, Dad." Jenny's seat belt clicked, the door whispered open and he was alone with the bovine. Rather damp lips that smelled like grass came dangerously close to his wristwatch. His oldest daughter came to the rescue with a gentle, "Come here, girl."

He took notes in case there was a next time, as the three human females led the throng of cows away. His neurotransmitters fired haphazardly, which had to be the reason he couldn't look away from Cheyenne. The side-view mirror framed her perfectly as she walked with her hand on the bull's neck, chatting merrily to the animals and to his daughters.

What was it about the woman? Why couldn't he look away?

She paused at the green truck parked behind him and rummaged around in the backseat. She was a splash of colors, auburn hair, sun-bronzed skin, green T-shirt, denim jeans and she claimed something deeper within him he could not name.

He didn't remember getting out of the car. Suddenly he was standing on the pavement with the Wyoming wind ruffling his hair, squinting against the sun, spellbound by her brightness. Cheyenne Granger tossed her head, her chuckle a soft melodic sound that rippled through the air and seemed to make the daisies in the field stand up to take notice.

He couldn't explain what ached deep inside

as if he'd contracted organ failure. He could not breathe as Cheyenne marched right through the herd, a slip of a woman compared to those large and powerful animals. His daughters trailed in her wake, Julianna skipping, her face beaming. He hadn't realized how happy staying the summer in Wyoming was making his girls. Jenny laughed, actually *laughed* right along with Cheyenne as the girl climbed down the embankment into the knee-high grass, a different child from the one she'd been a month ago.

"Cheyenne! I think Shrek loves me." Julianna wrapped her arms around the bull's broad chest.

Concern lurched through him as he launched forward, but the huge animal nibbled at one of Julianna's pigtails affectionately. Adam skidded to a stop, feeling awkward on the side of the road.

"He is definitely sweet on you." Cheyenne strong-armed the heavy bag to the ground and bent to move aside the wires of what used to be a working fence. "Jenny, looks like you've found some new friends, too."

"As if." The tween rolled her eyes, hiding a giggle as several cows vied for her affection. With her dark hair framing her face, she looked as sweet as the little girl she used to be and grown-up enough to show the hint of the woman she would become one day. Kind and thoughtful and gentle-hearted. He was grateful the Lord had led him here.

"All right, you bunch of troublemakers." Humor rang like a song as Cheyenne tore open the bag and waded into the tall grasses. "Look what I have for you."

Every cow's head lifted, and big nostrils scented the breeze. Ears pricked upward. Eyes brightened. The animals clattered around Jenny and lipped at Julianna's pigtails on the way by, streaming down the embankment and through the hole in the fence, Shrek in the lead.

"Nothing like a little bribery." Cheyenne upended the last of the bag, gave it a shake and stepped back as the herd descended on the pile of treats. Teeth crunched, jowls worked and tails swished as the cows happily ate. Cheyenne tracked back to the red fence posts, rounded up the girls and sent them climbing the embankment before she restrung the wire the best she could, considering the fence posts were leaning.

"Daddy, did you see?" Julianna rushed up, pleasure pinked her cheeks. "I love cows and they love me."

Don't even start. The words rang in his mind and formed on his tongue. We're not getting a cow. But his daughter's shining joy stopped him.

"I want to be just like Cheyenne when I grow up." She grabbed his hand, her fingers small compared to his, so very small. Her pigtails were askew and tiny bits of grass were embedded in the soft brown hair. Her summery shirt had a big wet spot from some cow's adoring lick. She tipped her head, chatting on merrily. "I'm gonna be a vet so I can fix birds like Tomasina and take care of dogs like Cheyenne does and so I can find every lonely animal their very own home."

"I'm sure you will be very good at it." He remembered what dreams were, so precious like twinkling stars that gave light to a vast night of darkness, dreams that could shine so bright if fed with hope and encouragement.

What had happened to his dreams? Where had they gone?

"Aunt Cady's not going to believe it happened again, that more cows were on the road." Jenny bounded up to the car door and yanked it open. "I get to tell her first this time, Julianna. You always do it and it's my turn."

"I do not," Julianna argued gleefully. "Okay, maybe I do but I don't mean to. It just comes out. I can't stop it."

"Well, try." Feigning annoyance, Jenny rolled her eyes and plopped onto the backseat.

Adam felt a tug of awareness, the realization that Cheyenne Granger was near. Vaguely, he noticed Julianna release his hand, scamper away and climb in beside her sister. He reached for his open door, finding his knees a little iffy. Weak knees, damp palms—the woman was a hazard to him.

"The cows are safely contained for now, although how long that patch job holds is anyone's guess." Cheyenne padded toward him in hiking boots, and he realized the shirt she wore had Wild Horse Animal Hospital scrawled across it in looping white letters. "I called the Parnells, so one of them should be out in a jiffy to do a better job with that fence. They send their apologies for inconveniencing you."

"I didn't know what to do. Next time I will." Near to her, he felt awkward, too tall, too big and too dark, as if the sunlight didn't touch him. "Honking didn't seem to work."

"Goodness, no!" She laughed. "That only made them more curious. I don't know why cows are so fascinated by the road, but most times when they get out they don't head for the hills kicking up their heels and enjoying their freedom. They stand in the road."

"I noticed."

"I suppose if I was a cow in a field watching the traffic go by, I might want to go where all the action is, too." She looked down at the crumpled and empty feed bag she still clutched, as if it held answers for her there— or perhaps he was making her feel awkward again.

Yes, that was it. He was staring at her too much. Definitely too much. He cleared his throat and turned his attention to the cattle. A few vied for the last of the treats while the rest of the herd had turned around and noted the gap in the fence had been repaired. Sorrowful moos rang out and several animals leaned against the wire.

"Isn't it supposed to be electric?" he asked. "Shouldn't that hurt?"

"Tall grass must have short-circuited the current somewhere. It happens." She shrugged, taking a step backward. "You probably don't run into this problem very often in midtown Manhattan."

"Can't say that I do." She was funny, he realized, and almost smiled. "You have quite a skill when it comes to cattle."

"I've been around them all my life. You've met my dad. He grew up on our family ranch just like I did. My earliest memories are being in the barns with him, walking between the stalls, going from animal to animal doling out treats, food, formula and medical care as needed."

"It must have been a nice way to grow up."

"It was. God incredibly blessed me with the life I have." Love for her life, that was something that would never change. She shook her head at the cows leaning over the fence, begging with their Bambi eyes and tragic moos for more of those yummy treats. She held up the empty bag so they could see. "That's all I have. No more."

They surely recognized the words *no more.* The cows appeared shocked at how that could possibly be true, and then even more sad as their moos began again.

"Persistence is the key to more treats," she explained. "Every pampered animal knows it."

"I look at you and see what I'm in for. Julianna just told me she wants to be a vet."

He must mean it kindly, but it was hard to tell from the stoic expression etched on his granite face.

"A vet? Well, that is a noble calling. It's the best way to spend your life, in my humble opinion. Taking care of animals all day, every day. Complete and total heaven." She flashed him a smile because he looked as if he needed one. Maybe he didn't realize his wounds were showing; then again, she had a knack for sensing them.

"Guess I will see you all at home." She tossed him an encouraging smile. "Mrs. G. has been cooking and baking up a storm. Her sons were all too busy for her to visit, so she's spending the holiday with us, and can she cook! It will be a treat, I promise."

"Dad." The window rolled down, and Jenny poked out her head. "How much longer? Can we go yet?"

"Patience, Jennifer."

He would have sounded gruff except for the faint twinkle in the doctor's eyes—really amazing brown eyes.

Not that she should be noticing. Adam Stone wasn't as dour as he wanted everyone to think as he turned those dazzling eyes on her.

"Thanks for clearing the road." He held his hand up to shade his eyes. "You may have saved my car from serious damage."

"No problem. I noticed just a little spittle, nothing to worry about." She backed away, long locks bouncing. "If this ever happens again, and in this part of the country it probably will, don't let them near your car. They can be quite enthusiastic."

"I noticed."

"Get out and lead them off the road. It helps

if you have something for them to eat. Oh, and call the sheriff. Ford Sherman knows how to deal with them. He was a city boy and he learned. I imagine you can be taught, too."

"Me, taught? That is one rumor never proven to be true," he quipped, surprised by the flutter of lightheartedness behind his sternum.

"I have faith in you, Adam." She climbed into her dark green truck and the tinted windshield hid all but the faintest silhouette of her behind the wheel, lovely and brilliant and amazing.

Not that he thought so on a personal level. It was merely an observation.

"Dad! We're waiting," Jenny called out the window. "It's getting hot sitting here."

"Yeah, Dad," Julianna chimed in. "Aunt Cady said we were going on a horse ride. She promised they wouldn't leave without us. It's gonna be a real trail ride!"

The green pickup passed in the oncoming lane with a toot of the horn and a wave of one slender hand. He couldn't move or respond as he watched Cheyenne's truck go by, engine rumbling, equipment in the bed rattling, the trailer hitch glinting as it caught on a ray of sun.

He was in shadow. Life had become incredibly serious and the wounds from living had cut deep. He felt darker as Cheyenne's pickup pulled into the lane ahead of him and rolled farther away. Over the past few years, he'd been consumed with the demands of running a household, raising his kids and meeting the challenges of his career. He hadn't stopped to think about the man he had become.

He didn't like who he was turning out to be. He'd lost hope, he'd lost touch with his soul, he'd forgotten what living was for.

Sunshine tumbled merrily across brilliant green pastures dotted with daisies. The cows across the road chorused a string of pleading moos in one last-ditch effort for attention. Life was big and his spirit had become so small. He wasn't quite sure when that had happened.

How did I get off track, Lord?

Sorry for it, he folded his six-foot-plus frame behind the wheel, closed the door and followed the ribbon of winding country road, fearing the answers he would get to that question.

Chapter Four

"Cheyenne! Cheyenne!" Julianna bolted from the sedan the moment the car rolled to a stop. She hopped and skipped like a purple butterfly across the gravel. "Are you gonna go on the trail ride, too?"

"That's the word." The girl looked so excited, that if she kept hopping like that she might rocket off the earth and take off into orbit. "Dad and Scotty promised they would have the horses saddled and ready to go by the time I stepped foot back on the ranch. And guess what? Both of my feet are on Granger land."

"So, what horse do I get to ride? Do you know?" Julianna bopped around, hopping backward, to keep an eye on her older sister and her father who were following at a normal pace.

"It's a surprise." She could not forget the shadows she'd seen in the man, although they were hard to see now in the full light of the sun as he gave Jenny a tight smile and clicked his remote to lock his car.

"Who are you expecting to steal your car?" she called out, unable to resist. "One of the cows?"

"Actually, you look a little shifty." He slid dark glasses onto his nose, hiding the humor threatening to sparkle in his eyes.

She laughed. The doctor was definitely not as dour as he seemed. "Yes, the time I spent out of state at vet school was a ruse to hide my notorious stint as a car thief."

"You may have everyone in this town fooled, but not me." He almost smiled again, that handsome half hook in the corners of his mouth.

Handsome? Was she really using that word *again?* She needed to stop thinking about him like that. Honestly. It wasn't as if she were in the market for a boyfriend. She rolled her eyes and accompanied Julianna around the bend in the walkway. The backyard came into sight, shaded by the big maple where her family waited, sprawled out in chairs and chaises, taking it easy for a change.

"There she is. About time, too." Dad launched off a patio chair on the shady grass. "We've been waiting on you, girl."

"And on us, too!" Julianna hoppity-hopped

to Cady and gave her an enthusiastic hug. "Guess what? Jenny changed her clothes eight times and there was a whole herd of—"

"Cows!" Jenny interrupted as she marched into sight a few steps ahead of her father. "Julianna, you promised I could tell."

"Oops. Sorry. I forgot."

The sisters were too cute. Cheyenne headed up the porch step. "I so relate to you, Jenny. I had a little sister not so different from Julianna."

"I was a cutie-patootie, wasn't I?" Addy bounced off the picnic table where she'd been sitting. Dimples framed her grin as she turned her attention to Julianna. "Adorable, sweet as pie, a real keeper. That was me."

"Not me." Julianna wiggled away from Cady's hug and grabbed her dad's hand. "I'm nothing but trouble."

"That's what you are, little girl." Adam tugged a bouncy brown pigtail, his affection showing through the stony cast to his features. "Trouble. I'm thinking of packing you up and taking you to the post office."

"Will you mail me to Hawaii?"

"That's not far away enough. I was thinking Antarctica."

"I think there are penguins there. That would be okay." She tilted her head to glimmer up at her father and there was no mistaking the depths of the child's adoration.

Cheyenne swallowed hard, remembering looking up at her dad just like that when the man had been so impossibly tall, a giant to her little-girl self, her true anchor in the world. He still was.

"Are you ready to roll, missy?" Her father's hand settled on her shoulder, a light but comforting weight that made her feel cozy and safe. That was her dad, always taking care of his kids, even if they were all grown-up. He leaned in with concern. "You aren't going to stay here in case a call comes in, are you?"

"No, I'm taking my cell with me. I can't miss a Granger family trail ride." She dropped her bag beside the bench and stole her Stetson off a wall peg.

"The family is a mite bigger than last year." Dad sounded pleased with that. "Hey, Hattie! What are you still doing in the kitchen?"

"Just packing up a bag of treats for the trail." Cheerful and sixtyish, Mrs. Gunderson zipped the Baggie she'd just filled with snickerdoodles and stuffed it into the saddlebag lying on the kitchen island. "I don't want anyone getting hungry. I put in a few treats for the little tykes.

Now, if you just want to take this with you, Frank, I'll get the thermoses to Cheyenne."

"You are coming with us, right, Mrs. G.?" Cheyenne did her duty and snatched the two silver thermoses from the counter.

"Lass, I don't belong on the back of a horse. No, my place is right here on solid ground." A smile wreathed her apple-dumpling face and twinkled in her gray eyes. "I've got a few things to do in the kitchen and then I'll be happy to put my feet up in the shade for a spell."

"Not gonna happen." Dad flashed his dimples at her. "You're an honorary member of this family and we don't leave family behind."

"I've never ridden a horse and I don't aim to start today." Mrs. G. handed over the pack. "No, I'll be waiting right here when you get back."

"That's not the way this is gonna work." Her dad glanced at her for help. "What's your opinion, Cheyenne?"

"If you don't go, Mrs. G., I don't go."

"That's not what I want at all." Distress crinkled prettily on her round face, enhancing her soft beauty. "You go along, Cheyenne."

"No, I'll stay and keep you company. Addy will, too." She knew Mrs. G. had a special fondness for the youngest of the Granger clan. "She was really counting on taking you riding, but I guess she will have to be disappointed."

"Very disappointed," Dad piped in.

"Oh, you two do not play fair." Mrs. G.'s gaze strayed to the big picture windows where the family and friends gathered at the edge of the lawn. Saddled horses were tied to a rail fence, and a half dozen cattle lowed on their side of the field, begging for attention. Addy had Julianna by one hand and six-year-old Owen by the other, walking between the horses, chattering away.

Adam. He stood like a statue a safe distance away from the horses, the chiseled wonder of his masculine face furrowed with unmistakable apprehension. Cady closed in on him, making conversation. Ooh, what she would give to be a fly on the fence post so she could hear them. Had he just realized that Scotty their ranch hand had saddled a horse for him, too?

"Life isn't fair, Hattie, and I aim to do whatever it takes." Dad tossed the saddlebag over his shoulder like a Western hero of old and headed for the door. "You come along with us. You'll have a good time. You have my word."

"I'm holding you to that, Frank Granger." But an interested twinkle sparkled in her eyes.

"It's settled, then." Pleased, Dad strolled out

onto the porch. His gaze arrowed to Cady and the love that took him over was a sight to see. His deep, abiding affection for Cady shone too brightly to hide.

"Lass, will you show me what to do?" Mrs. G. followed down the stairs.

"I may have my hands full with another greenhorn." Why was she smiling? It was because of the adamant way Adam shook his head. His no-way-are-you-getting-me-on-a-horse manner made her chuckle. She winked at Mrs. G. "At least you won't be the only first-timer. You may have to set a good example for the new doctor in town."

"Cheyenne! Cheyenne!" Julianna bolted across the lawn, running full-out. "Guess what? Dusty and Princess are here. Frank trailered them over from the inn. We get to ride 'em!"

"You look happy." The homeless and abused horses that the inn had taken on were thriving, thanks to cousin Sean and his fiancée Eloise's care and the Stone girls' pampering. Two of the horses had taken a shine to each of the girls. Seeing the way the golden mare lifted her head to always keep an eye on little Julianna spoke of a growing bond. She gave a light tug on one of Julianna's ponytails. "Do you think you can show Mrs. G. how to mount up?"

"I sure can! It's real easy."

"Oh, is that a good idea?" the housekeeper asked, dimpled and merry. "She's such a little girl."

"With a big heart, and besides, she knows how to ride." Cheyenne felt Adam's gaze land on her like a touch to her chin. Her skin buzzed with a strange sensation. Maybe a bug had landed there. She rubbed her jawbone but nothing flew away.

"Don't worry, Hattie. I'll help, too," Scotty called out from beside an older bay mare, the gentlest horse in the Granger inventory.

"All right, then." Mrs. G. chuckled as Julianna pulled her away.

She ought to be joining her family, reining Wildflower down the trail, leading the way. She should be contributing to the family's merry conversation and banter, but they seemed incredibly far away. Adam stood front and center, a few safe paces away from the few remaining horses. With the brush of the wind through his dark thick locks and the kiss of the sun on his bronzed complexion, he appeared intensely male and as polished as if he'd just walked off the covers of an outdoors magazine.

Not that she was attracted to that. Puzzling how she kept noticing him.

"Daddy, you haven't got in your saddle yet."

Julianna's button face lined with worry. "Don't you know how?"

"Sure I do." He straightened his spine, becoming more tall and powerful.

The fact that her heart kicked into an alarming arrhythmia was a complete coincidence. In fact, she wasn't going to wait on a city boy like Adam Stone. She strolled over to Wildflower and rubbed her nose. Her old friend nickered softly, bumping her velvety nose into Cheyenne's hand in an obvious request for more petting. Hard to refuse that. She leaned her forehead against Wildflower's cheek and savored the sweet company her mare offered.

"I guess staying here and reading the book I have in the car is out of the question." Adam's deep baritone held a chord of emotion—a note of amusement and a softer one of resignation.

"Dad, that's so not what you agreed to do." Jenny's dark gaze held a plea, one mirrored by her younger sister.

Not that the Stone family dynamics were any of her business, but she'd grown fond of the girls and she couldn't seem to keep her attention away from the man. He was a good father. He might be thinking the stoic cast to his face came across as stern, but she could read the affection for his daughters beneath the surface and the look of love that said how much he wanted to please his girls.

Glimmers of admiration flared to life within her as she patted Wildflower's neck. So, she was a softy for a man with a good heart. She liked him despite all the reasons she shouldn't. He was remote, he was abrupt and she got the strong impression he didn't like small-town life or country living. She couldn't fault him for the look of trepidation he gave the waiting horse. He kept back, apparently mostly clueless what to do with the animal.

"Should I help him, Wildflower?" she asked her beloved mare. "What do you think?"

Wildflower nickered, her chocolate gaze approving of the man.

"All right, fine," Cheyenne whispered. "But if it doesn't work out, it's your fault."

Wildflower nodded, apparently good with that. Cheyenne patted the mare's sun-warmed flank as she circled over to lend Adam a hand. He definitely looked as if he could use it. The poor man squinted at Scout, one of her brother's horses, as if getting up on that gelding was about as appealing as catching a case of the bird flu.

"Look at Mrs. G." She nodded toward the long line of horses and riders mounting up.

"She's never been on a horse before and she's having a lot of fun."

"I don't do fun."

"True, but you could fake it just this once."

"I know what you're trying to do." He glanced over just in time to see the housekeeper give a hoot of surprise as the ranch hand gave her a boost into the saddle.

"Way to go, Mrs. G.!" Cheyenne cheered.

The older woman rose up in the air, swung her leg over the back of the horse and landed in the saddle with a surprised plop. "Oh, my! This is much higher than I thought. How do I keep from sliding right off?"

"First you need to wear this." Scotty handed up Autumn's extra Stetson, which he must have thought to bring from the barn.

Was that a sparkle of interest in Scotty's gaze? The strapping ranch hand, also in his sixties, leaned in, lowered his voice and gave Mrs. G. a bit of advice.

"If she can do it, I'm sure you can." Cheyenne sidled up to Adam. "It's not difficult. Honestly."

"For you, sure. You're one of those animal people. You've probably ridden a horse since before you could walk."

"True, but I'll help you out. How about that?" The turn of the corners of her pretty rosebud mouth *could* have been meant to tease him, but the kindness glimmering quietly in her bright blue gaze did not.

"Daddy, please?" Julianna clasped her hands together, steepled as if in prayer. There had been so much he hadn't been able to give her over the past few years—her mother's return to their family, her mother's full-time interest and a way to make her pain ease. But this he could do. His daughter wanted him to go on a horse ride with her. How could he say no?

Remembering his single, very bad experience with a horse when he was a boy, how could he say yes?

"Dad saddled up Scout for you. Scout is a real gentleman." Cheyenne probably thought she was reassuring him as she led the way toward the horses, her light auburn hair spilling over her shoulder. "Don't worry. It will be a piece of cake."

Sure, like last time. He tried to erase the images rising into his mind like a DVD player in slow motion. The pony baring his teeth and snapping as he tried to mount. The nick of teeth stinging his upper arm. Squaring his shoulders, he took one step forward toward the few horses still tied to the rail. Most folks had mounted up and the big crowd of Grangers were milling around, saddles creaking, steeled hooves striking the ground, all eyes on him.

He probably looked like a coward, or at the very least a disagreeable man who didn't know how to have fun. He felt the shadows within him. Fun wasn't something he'd been inclined to have since the divorce, when life had become incredibly serious.

"Dad, this will be so much fun. You'll see." Jenny, more child than teenager at the moment, loped ahead of him with deerlike grace. "You can ride with me."

"Uh-huh, he's gonna ride with me!" Julianna argued cheerily from atop her little gold mare.

"The trail is wide enough that he can ride with both of you." Cheyenne cheerfully untied reins from the fence board. A cow rambled up to investigate, a daisy stuck in the tuft of hair between her ears, something his girls must have done. "I wish you could come along, too, Buttercup, but you'll have to stay here."

The bovine had a similar pleading gaze as Julianna, wide eyes and hopes impossible to disappoint.

"I'm sorry, girlfriend." Cheyenne stroked the cow's wide nose before turning to him. "Are you ready to saddle up?"

He was more inclined to take off at a dead run, but cowardice had never been a flaw of his. If only so many gazes weren't tracking his progress as he strode up to the horse, the menace on four legs. At least, that was his memory of being on horseback.

It will be better this time. That was the only thought that kept the fear at bay. *Lord, I hope this isn't a disaster,* he added in prayer, because he would need all the help he could get.

The big behemoth studied him with friendly cocoa eyes. The horse's nostrils rounded as he breathed in and out in a low-throated sound that could have been a growl.

Man up, he told himself but he couldn't stop the DVD player part of his brain. The memory froze in this exact spot when he'd been four at his own birthday party. His heart had been pounding then, too, from excitement, not an impending sense of doom. But instead of the grizzled old man holding the reins, Cheyenne posed beside him, awash with sunshine and beauty, looking like everything good in the world.

"Does he bite?" It didn't hurt to ask.

"I've never known him to, but for you he might make an exception." She must think she was being funny.

He couldn't bring himself to tell her the truth. He swallowed hard and stepped up to the saddle. He had to reach up to the saddle horn, but not too far. That was one advantage of being tall. He feared the disadvantage might be the old adage, the taller they are, the harder they fall.

"Look at Mrs. G." Cheyenne, determined to encourage him, nodded in the direction of the cluster of horses and riders on the gravel lane. The older lady balanced in the saddle, clutching the saddle horn with both hands.

"I hear what you're saying." He wasn't about to be outdone by a woman twice his age. His masculine pride proved to be stronger than his old fear. He lifted his foot and slipped it into the stirrup, gave a hop and rose into the saddle.

"Hey, you're an old pro at this." Cheyenne beamed up at him, respect softening her fantastic blue eyes. Her irises had little flecks of aquamarine in them and darker threads of navy blue. His heart skipped.

Probably it had to do with the adrenaline spiking through his system. He settled into the saddle, fit his other boot into the stirrup and held out his hands for the reins. "It's not my first time."

"So, you don't need my help?"

"I didn't say that." The force of her kindness made him forget for a moment everything but the feel of the sun on his back and the way the summer breeze played with the bouncy ends of her auburn hair. The world became so bright it hurt the eye. Stunning sunshine, lush vivid green grasses, nodding daisies, the sky bluer than her gaze.

"I'll stick close," she promised, waltzing away like a summer song and bopped from the ground to the back of her horse with the grace of a gymnast. She tipped back her Stetson and gathered the reins in one hand. "Let's head out, Dad!"

The riders and their horses headed toward the tree line, following the fence that marched through wild meadows. An access road cut a narrow swatch between fenced fields where horses grazed on one side and cattle drowsed in shade on the other. He really wanted to believe this horse-riding thing was going to work out, if only he could forget the past.

For a moment, seated awkwardly on the horse, clutching the saddle horn he remembered the boy he'd been, trying to ignore his smarting arm where the pony had bitten him and wanting to ride like a cowboy in his favorite movies. Except instead of taking the first step, the pony had let out a terrifying squeal and began bucking. All these years later, he could remember the sensation of flying out of that saddle.

But he caught sight of his girls. At the corner

fence post, they were waiting for him along with the rest of the family. Jenny, astride the brown mare she'd taken a liking to, squinted at him through the brightness. Julianna sat on the little golden mare like a pro, reins in one hand. Both girls watched him with adoration, as if he'd hung the moon just for them.

As if he could disappoint them.

He patted Scout's velvet warm neck, feeling the strength of the animal beneath him. Muscles flexed, the horse's weight shifted as he waited impatiently for the command to go. Now, what did he do? Adam had no clue. Standing still had never been a problem for the pony.

"Come on, Scout." Cheyenne clucked her tongue Western-style. As her white-and-gold horse stepped out to join the others, so did Scout.

He lurched in the saddle, unaccustomed to the strange, swaying movement. He tried to stop the memory but there was no pause button for his gray matter. His neurons continued to flash backward to that dreadful moment thirty years ago when the pony had its first step. His head had gone down, his rear went up and the little boy he'd once been had flown into the gravel.

Not going to happen this time, he told himself, adding a *Please be merciful, Lord* just in case. Scout's head stayed up and his rear remained where it belonged as the horse lifted his long, powerful legs and followed the others. Adam gave thanks for that. There was no terrifying squeal. No projectile flying out of his saddle. No hitting the ground with enough force to break his wrist.

Yet.

"How's it going?" Cheyenne and her mare caught up to him. Not a hint of amusement rang in her voice, which he appreciated.

"So far so good."

"I wouldn't have teased you, if I'd known." She tipped up the brim of her hat to peer at him, purely at ease in the saddle. "You are deathly afraid of horses."

"What gave me away?"

"I've never seen such a white-knuckled grip." She gestured at his hands, which were nearly bloodless, proof he held on to both the reins and the saddle horn for dear life.

"Neither have I," he admitted, surprised at the chuckle almost rising in his chest, something he hadn't felt in a long, long time. It made it easier to try to relax in the saddle and enjoy the ride. The scenery was spectacular enough to speak to his soul.

Chapter Five

It was hard to know what on earth to say to the man. She hadn't yet figured him out. He seemed content to ride along in silence. Did he feel out of place among them? Or was he starting to like the experience? She couldn't stay quiet for long. "You're doing pretty good for a greenhorn."

"It's not my first time on a horse." His gaze was impossible to read behind his high-end sunglasses. A muscle ticked in his granite jaw. "It is the first time I've stayed in the saddle."

"I've learned there's a big difference between the two."

"So have I."

He almost smiled again. The rocky set to his features softened, the serious line of his mouth eased and the effect stole her breath.

Good thing she had sworn off men or she might develop the tiniest crush on him.

"Your death grip has eased up. Are you starting to enjoy the ride?"

"Not yet, but I'm hopeful." A dash of humor warmed the cool tones of his voice.

"Me, too. I hope that you get to experience what your daughters are feeling." She nodded ahead to the girls who rode side by side, their happy chatter and laughter floating on the wind like lark song. "It's why they like it here."

"Trust me, I already know. They like the horses and all the new amusements. Once it's no longer as novel, the luster will wear off. I'm hoping that will happen before school starts, so I won't have much trouble getting them back home again."

"It sounds as if you have it all figured out."

"I always do." His voice turned to steel. He squared his already-straight shoulders, remote and unreachable again.

She hoped he was right. The riding party had thinned out over the past two miles. Justin and his wife, Rori, led the pack and were so far ahead she could no longer catch sight of them on the pleasantly curving path through the trees. Sean and his fiancée, Eloise, were barely visible through the stands of evergreens. She caught a swish of Pixie's white tail before the mare disappeared from sight and so did the happy couple. Autumn and Ford were next, the newlyweds who rode side by side holding hands. They radiated the kind of contentment only written about in fairy tales. It was nice to see.

Addy kept pace with Scotty and Mrs. G.; the faint lift and fall of her voice as she chattered away was nothing more than the faintest murmur made small by the grand panorama of vast blue sky, green foothills and the miles upon miles of lowland. The craggy peaks of the Tetons bordered the western horizon with stunning and majestic grace.

She definitely loved it here. She belonged on this land. She was thankful to live here surrounded by family and friends. Judging by the Stone girls a few paces ahead, she guessed they might feel the same way. The two sisters talked low to each other, looking captivated by the wonders surrounding them. It was the first time the city girls had been up in the foothills. Easy to see they loved the adventure.

"Cheyenne! Look!" Julianna pointed up at the sky. "Another hawk circling."

"Yep. Looks like a daddy hunting for his family's supper." She tipped back her head, hand on her hat, to glance up at the graceful hawk. He sailed like poetry high in the sky.

Pretty awesome, in her opinion. "If you keep your eyes peeled, you might even see a deer or an elk. I see tracks."

"We've seen lots of deer in Cady's fields, but not an elk." Jenny whipped her head around, checking on both sides of the trail where lacy green boughs could hide glimpses of wild animals. "Seeing an elk would be cool."

"Are there any cougar tracks, Cheyenne?" Julianna twisted in her saddle, glittering at the possibility. "Do you see any?"

"Not that I've noticed from this high up," she quipped, feeling as light as the wind swishing by. Wildlife enchanted her, too. "When we stop, you and I can search along the creek for tracks. Does that sound fun? We're more likely to find cat tracks there, where a cougar might stop to get a drink."

"Daddy, did you hear? We're going to search for a cougar." Julianna bounced in her saddle, so excited. When her sister pointed, the two stood in their stirrups straining to see a jackrabbit bounding through the underbrush.

"So you think this excitement will wear off over time?" Cheyenne couldn't help asking.

"I'm praying it does, otherwise when the summer ends there are going to be two very unhappy little girls in my house." Wry, he shrugged, perhaps unaware he looked in the direction of the disappearing jackrabbit, too. "I'm not sure how I'm going to pry them off those horses."

"Or away from Cady?" She hadn't missed how attached the Stone girls had become to their honorary aunt. Cady, who'd never had children of her own, was devoted to them although right now, she was pretty absorbed in a conversation with Dad.

"Especially from Cady." Adam dropped his voice and leaned closer. "She has filled a void in my daughters' lives where their mother used to be."

"Cady is wonderful. They couldn't have a better void filler." She went for humor to ease away from the emotions she felt rising between them. She didn't want to look into Adam's private life; she didn't want to get that close to any guy.

"Cady has been great. She's one of the reasons the girls are doing as well as they are, considering the hard blow they took." He grew serious again, the square, unyielding line of his jaw turning to rock. "Cady told me the same thing happened to you when you were a child. Your mom left for selfish reasons."

"Yes, Mom was never happy being a rancher's wife. I think she wanted to be, she tried to be, but she didn't have it in her. The remoteness, the hard work and the fact that we think a trail ride is the epitome of a good time were all things that frustrated her." That time no longer hurt to think about, but once it had been like a terrible wound she feared would never heal. "It devastated me and my family the day she left."

"That's what happened to us." No emotion seemed to touch him, he could have been talking about the weather except for the cords tightening in his neck.

He was holding everything in, she suspected, just the way her dad had done. She had been a little younger than Julianna was but she clearly remembered the utter heartbreak her father had fought to hide. In her view there was no man stronger than Frank Granger, but having his wife leave the family for another man had cut him to the soul. He'd done his best to keep that private, but he'd been a changed man that day. He'd gotten over it, he'd done his best for his family but he had never trusted another woman. The shadow of Mom's betrayal did not fade from his eyes until Cady came along.

Cheyenne glanced over her shoulder, drawn to her dad. He was happy like he'd been in the old days, fully whole of heart. His Stetson shaded his face, the familiar rumble of his chuckle held only joy as he rode side by side with Cady. The pair seemed connected in heart and spirit on a level that was rare and heaven sent. The memory of that long-ago pain seemed gone, but she knew Adam had to be wrestling with something similar.

"How did it happen?" The instant the question was out, she regretted it. Not her business. The last thing Adam probably wanted was to discuss what hurt him most with a complete stranger. He looked as if he needed a friend, and she could sense his hurt. She had to help, if she were able. It was simply the way God had made her.

"You were thinking I must be hard to live with, weren't you?" The wryness faded, leaving only unreadable granite. "I won't say it wasn't true."

"Not what I was thinking. Honestly." She nudged Wildflower closer on the trail, bridging the distance between them. Now they were close enough to talk so their words would not carry to the girls up ahead. "I'm a good listener."

"I don't see the use in talking about it. Talking won't change what happened. It won't fix what's wrong now." He studied his daughters, merrily enjoying their ride. "Stacy was never happy in our marriage. She was never happy with me. Maybe things had been wrong between us right from the start. I don't honestly know. I was busy with med school and then vying for a top-tier residency. I did my best, but it wasn't good enough."

"Relationships can be tricky. That's why I stay away from them." Leather creaked pleasantly as she shifted in her saddle.

"Good idea. I wish I had been that smart."

"You look like a smart man to me."

"No, just fair to middling." At least as far as relationships were concerned. The answers necessary for them could not be found in a medical textbook. "Stacy was always restless in our life together. Having kids helped for a while, but as soon as Julianna was in grade school, the problems were worse. It turns out when I thought she was taking an art class, she was meeting my best friend at a ritzy hotel. Dumb me, I never guessed, not until she was already gone."

"The sudden shock of learning how very much she'd betrayed had to be rough." Sympathy softened the delicate angles of Cheyenne's face and made her heart show.

He'd never realized before how lovely that could make a woman. He swallowed hard, determined not to let his gaze stray toward her again. His palms went damp, his pulse arrhythmic. If this kept up, he would have to get an EKG.

"It was a stunning surprise. There was no real warning." He knew he should stay quiet, leave it at that. He'd spilled enough of his guts to this woman who was little more than a stranger. Except she didn't feel that way. He couldn't explain it. Maybe because she knew his daughters so well and obviously was good to them. Perhaps there was a deeper reason. He'd been a lonely man for a long time, bottling this up and refusing to talk. The words simply spilled out. "I came home to find the house empty. The girls were next door at the neighbors. Stacy's closet was mostly empty. She'd taken everything of value, jewelry, bonds, drained the savings account."

"No, she left what was most valuable behind." Cheyenne's correction came gently, but it hit him hard.

"Thank you for that." His voice sounded gruff with emotion, emotion he wasn't comfortable with. He wasn't used to personal comments. Surely Cheyenne Granger was being nice, that was all, but her kindness touched him deeply and he kept right on talking. "Of course, the girls were the greater treasure. Stacy sees them a few weekends when she feels like keeping to the schedule. She wasn't inclined to fund two round-trip tickets every other week, so she hasn't seen the girls in a while."

"Do they miss her?"

"Yes, but their visits with Stacy always upset them more."

"I remember when my mom came home again." Cheyenne winced, as if the memory was still sensitive.

He supposed some wounds always were. "Your mother came back?"

"She was sick. I don't know what happened with the man she left Dad for but when she needed something, she called Dad. He took her in and hired all the care she needed. He paid for everything and made sure she had every comfort."

Her incredibly expressive blue eyes radiated sorrow. Unlike him, she wasn't bitter and no walls closed her off. He admired that as she swallowed hard, as if preparing herself to say whatever was next.

"It nearly broke Dad to do it, but he said it was for us. So that we could make peace with her. She was our mom." She shrugged, and the pain faded from her eyes. "I was about Julianna's age. It was hard to learn that some people are unable to love and to give of themselves even to those who matter most. That doesn't make it your fault."

Emotion built up like a pressure behind his sternum and the walls he'd built around his heart inched down a notch. He'd never thought about it like that before. "I had my failings."

"Yes, but you weren't the one who left."

Her understanding so simply offered made him want to believe her. Her words were a balm to his long-standing sense of failure. Up ahead, his daughters burst into excited chatter.

"I saw one! I saw antlers and everything!" Julianna's pigtails bobbed as she bounced in the saddle. "Cheyenne, look! He's over there."

"Oh, I see. He's watching us from behind that old stump. He's handsome." Cheyenne swayed in her saddle, straining to get a good look.

Curious, he leaned to one side, gripping the saddle horn with all his strength, and peered between two pines into the dappled shadows. A regal elk, larger than a deer and as soft as brown velvet, watched them with wary eyes. Four-pronged antlers crowned his head.

Amazement washed through him. What surprised him most was the wonder he felt. He hadn't known he was capable of wonder anymore but it filled his chest with warmth, like a sunrise of his soul.

The wind puffed warmly across his face, rustling his hair, as if to remind him of the surrounding beauty. In life, he'd always kept his nose to the grindstone, working hard, doing what had to be done, focusing on his responsibilities. He wasn't so good at looking up. He couldn't remember the last time he'd taken a moment to enjoy the lazy warmth of summer sunshine. He breathed in the forest-scented wind and took a moment to listen to the music of the breeze through the trees, the pleasant rhythmic clomp of horse hooves on the earth and study the lay of the wild countryside that ranged from forest to lowland meadows. At the edge of his vision, Cheyenne swept off her hat and let the wind and sun spill over her.

Not going to notice, he told himself. His guard had lowered a bit, his defenses felt weakened and he knew she was to blame. She was the reason his lungs couldn't properly fill with air.

The moment passed, a curve in the trail took them out of sight of the elk, and he did his best not to notice the sheer drop-off on Cheyenne's side of the trail. He worried about his girls but the horses seemed sure-footed and calm, plodding along well away from the rocky edge. Still, he couldn't relax. That probably had more to do with the woman than the cliff.

"Do you think you will ever marry again?" Cheyenne's quiet question startled him.

"Marry?" He felt like one of the birds who spotted them and took off in a panicked flight.

"Don't worry. It wasn't a hint. I wasn't fishing." She plopped her hat back on her head and tossed him an amused smile. "I would rather throw myself down the embankment. Nothing personal. I'm sure you would be a fine catch, but I am not going down that path again. Not if I can help it."

"I know how you feel." He should have felt relieved. His pulse rate ought to be kicking back down to normal. Instead, he felt jittery and not only because of her question. "I can't see myself trusting another woman again."

"I understand. It took my dad sixteen years."

"The thing is, my girls need a real mom." He didn't know why he was telling her this, he didn't want to. Perhaps it was the caring gleam in her eyes. She enchanted animals big and small and she was doing the same to him. He was a human and should be able to use his reasoning powers to stop it, but not a single neuron fired. His brain was mush and his shields lowered further and the words rumbled off his tongue. "They need someone to be there when they come home from school. Someone to bake them cookies and take an interest in their ups and their downs. I'm not enough. I want to be, I try to be, but a father isn't a mother. I can fill in the gaps the best I can, but there's something elusive and valuable only a loving mother can provide."

"I think you are doing just fine. When we were young, Dad asked Aunt Opal to move in with us. She filled in the gaps, as you say. Now we have Mrs. G. Maybe you can find a housekeeper."

"I've thought of hiring a nanny type, but I feel my girls need more. I've prayed, but no solution has come to me."

"Maybe it will. You never know what God has in store for you."

Gazing into her compassionate gaze bluer than the Wyoming sky, he could feel the vulnerable places within him wish. Emotions too strong to measure and too varied to describe roared through him like a hurricane beating down his resolve, laying waste to his defenses. The woman was more than a danger to him. Defenseless, he could not stop the panic overtaking him. Being vulnerable to another woman on any level was too terrifying to risk. Even if it was only friendship.

His throat tightened in a spasm, nearly cutting off his ability to breathe. He knew Cheyenne meant well, she was only being nice and had taken a risk in being honest with him. He wished he could explain why he pressed his heels to the horse's sides and prayed the animal responded appropriately instead of bucking him off. He would rather hit the ground and roll down that endless embankment than to feel the wasteland his heart had become. The loneliness within him was too great and his shattered hopes too broken to look at in the light of day.

The horse leaped smoothly ahead, leaving Cheyenne behind in a cloud of fine dust.

"Daddy!" Julianna preened up at him, pleased he had come to ride beside her. Jenny did the same. They were his world and he relaxed as they chattered away, including him in their conversation.

He was aware of Cheyenne's puzzled silence behind him and the weight of her gaze on his back. A weight that remained all the way up the hillside, one he could not shake.

Cady Winslow leaned forward in her saddle as Misty crested the steep slope. She felt on top of the world, and with the way the high foothill peaked, leveling out in a grassy tree-fenced meadow, overlooking the valley below, she could fool herself into thinking she really was. The day wasn't over yet and already it had been one of the most enjoyable in her life. She was surrounded by friends and family, out in God's beautiful wilderness. Her Bible verse from her morning's devotional slipped into her mind.

By the word of the Lord the heavens were made, and all the host of them by the breath of His mouth. This is God's country, she decided as she let the rock and sway of her mare's gait lull her into a deep state of bliss. She had watched the golden rays brush at the treetops and burnish the rancher riding beside her. The golden light emphasized the brim of his hat, the handsome angle of his rugged jaw, his dependable, strapping shoulders and his powerful masculinity. Affection brighter than the sun swept through her, blinding her to all else. What was she going to do about her great and endless affection for Frank Granger?

"Looks like even the doctor is having a good time." Frank leaned in, keeping his baritone low. "I would call this a successful trail ride."

"Successful? How could it be a failure?"

"You just wait and see. The afternoon isn't over yet." Lapis-blue eyes snapped with humor, so incredibly blue and dreamy it could make a sensible woman like her, a woman who always did what was practical, forget to breathe. He patted the holstered rifle tied to his saddle. "I won't rule out bear, cougar or moose just yet."

"I hope we don't have any of that kind of trouble." She may have left her life in New

York over a year ago, but she still hadn't acclimated completely to rural Wyoming. "Is this really bear country? Should we be worried?"

"If we have trouble, it won't be my first." Confident, that was Frank. His understated, capable, laid-back strength appealed to her more every day. There was so much to admire about him, it would take her days to make a complete list. He drew his dark bay gelding to a halt and swung down. "I'll keep you safe, Cady."

That man could make her heart stop beating. True romance had always eluded her. A few men had been interested in her over the years when she'd been a Manhattan attorney, but nothing had lasted. She'd never clicked with any man the way she did with Frank.

"Besides, we haven't seen a bear up here in at least three summers." His sun-browned, callused hand closed over hers with a firm, commanding grip. Tingles skidded up her arm like little soda pop bubbles and were twice as sweet.

"It was two years, Dad." Tucker ambled over to take the horses. "Remember when we had a bear cub come after Addy's piece of huckleberry pie and his mama took offense?"

"Yep, that's right. That's why we no longer bring a picnic up here." Frank's fingers twined between hers and the bond between them felt like steel, unbreakable and enduring.

Don't think the L *word, Cady,* she told herself as she let him help her down from the saddle. It was a cozy feeling knowing he looked out for her, big and strong, her very own Western hero. She hardly noticed her feet were on the ground.

"Cheyenne!" A little girl's call rose above the rushing sounds of the wind, the drone of a lazy bee and birdsong. "You gotta come see!"

"Julianna is having a good time." Cady laughed, which was always so easy when she was with Frank. He adjusted his long-legged gait to match hers. She had to force her attention away from him to notice her surroundings. Tucker and Sean were picketing the horses, the Granger girls were clustered together chatting amicably and Adam looked lost, a shadow, dressed in black and standing apart from everyone.

He was out of his element. She had prayed he would find solace spending time with the Grangers, or at least have a little fun. She'd known him since he was a toddler when she'd babysat him. He'd always been serious and introverted. Stacy's treatment of him had only reinforced those traits. She wished she could do something to help fix his shattered heart.

"I'm glad you talked the doc into coming along." Frank stopped, keeping them a good distance from the others. Laughter rang and the conversation turned to discussing Mrs. Gunderson's first horseback ride. The draw of the happy group tugged at her. But as powerful as it was, nothing could compare to the magnetism of Frank's gaze capturing hers. "You never know when having a doctor around might come in handy."

"Especially where there are so many bears." Her quip fizzled as her heart forgot to beat again. His caring was a dream too real to be imagined and yet she could feel the truth of his affection all the way to her soul.

Love had never worked out for her. Every time she had gotten her hopes up, they had been dashed. Something had gone wrong. Either hers or the man's feelings had changed. Whatever happened she had been left alone and disappointed. That's why she couldn't allow herself to leap ahead or to wish for what could be with Frank. If this didn't work out, she would be so crushed there would be no recovering from it. No man had ever meant as much, not even close.

Just stay in the moment, she told herself as she fell into his gaze. His quiet adoration was enough. She would not dare hope for more.

"I'm glad you came along, too." His hat brim bumped hers. "I know that inn of yours is busy this weekend."

"I have a good staff, plus I bribed them by tripling their wage to cover me for the holiday weekend." As if she would have missed this moment with him. She had spent her whole adult life working while time passed, wishing for a connection like this. Now that she had it, she would savor every moment. Whatever lay ahead, she would always have this second, this minute, this day spent with Frank to remember.

"I'm grateful you don't mind spending your time with me." A bashful smile hooked the corners of his lean mouth.

"I don't mind. Much." Tenderness threatened to wash through her as sustaining and as beautiful as the light from above, but she held it in check. This was the moment she wanted to remember, just this sweet moment in time, as Frank leaned in, slanted his mouth over hers and kissed her sweetly.

Never had a kiss been more reverent or gentle. Cady curled her fingers into his shirt, glad when his arms circled her waist because the earth tilted and she felt unsteady. His strength kept her balanced and breathless against him. She didn't want his kiss to end.

"Eek!" Addy's distant squeal penetrated the misty reaches of her consciousness. "Bees!"

"Bees!" More voices joined in.

"It's always something." Frank broke the kiss but his arms continued to hold her tight. Regret crinkled attractively in the corners of his eyes and the shine of affection remained. Such a deep kind of affection. An answering well of caring filled her up and left her unable to speak.

Please, don't let this end, she prayed, unable to move away from him. Laughter rose above the shrieks and the commotion, men's voices joined in, for all she knew a horde of angry killer bees were zeroing in on her. Did she care?

Not a bit. What mattered most stood right in front of her, his dreamy blue eyes searching hers. In spite of the chaos, calm filled her.

Just enjoy the moment, she told herself. Every minute spent with Frank was the most precious she had ever known.

Chapter Six

"There's a finch." Julianna froze in the dappled shade of the small creek, peering upward toward the languidly rustling leaves.

"Looks like she's finding an early supper for her chicks." Cheyenne craned her neck as she balanced at the water's edge. The cheerful gurgle of the current tumbled over rocks and swished around eddies of earth. Little creatures skiddled above and beneath the surface, dashing away. Tiny fish, katydids, dragonflies. She would point them out to Julianna, but movement out of the corner of her eye stopped her.

Adam. He strode away from the crowd seated in the shade, his walk powerful and his expression dark, or maybe it was simply the effect that he wore nothing but black on this bright, perfect day. The cheerful nod of daisies at his feet and the rustle of Indian paintbrush as he swept by made him seem hewn of shadows and darkness, this man who had abruptly ridden away from her without a word. His walls had gone up, his friendliness had vanished and he hadn't looked at her again.

She wanted to be angry or insulted or in the very least annoyed, but she wasn't.

"What kind of footprints are these?" A musical little voice echoed at the far edge of her consciousness. "Cheyenne?"

"Deer." She shook her head, trying to scatter her thoughts of the man but they stuck like glue. How she managed to arrow her attention to the earthen bank was a total mystery. "See these littler hooves? A mom and her twins came to drink here not long ago."

"Really? How long ago?" Excited, Julianna dropped down, her pigtails dangling as she studied the tracks cut into the damp dirt. "Maybe they aren't very far away and we could see them."

"Maybe, maybe not. It's hard to know. Although if I were a mama deer, this meadow would be a peaceful place to let my fawns nap. Or it was until we came along."

"Do you see any other tracks?"

"You tell me." She rocked back on her heels, aware of Adam as he approached the horses.

She didn't know why her senses were tuned to him. Bewildering.

"These belong to a bird who was hopping around." Julianna seemed pleased. "Maybe it was a finch like Tomasina. Do you think she can go back to her home soon?"

"It looks that way. When I checked in with Ivy last, she said our little bird was doing well. Eating up a storm and standing up to flap her wings."

"God must have heard my prayer." Julianna swiped a flyaway strand of dark hair from her soulful eyes. "My dad says we aren't supposed to pray for ourselves, because that would be selfish."

"I do know God doesn't want us to think only of ourselves. He wants us to put others first." She couldn't stop her attention from drifting to the man. Alone, he was searching through Scout's saddlebags. When he pulled out a small first-aid kit, she realized he must be about to treat Jenny's bee sting. Maybe Addy's, too.

"I don't want to be selfish like my mom." As if she had put a lot of thought into this, Julianna's face scrunched up and she rested her chin on her fist. "I have some things I want to ask God for, but my Dad wouldn't like it."

"Like what?" The question was out before

she could stop it. She could sense Adam striding closer. She didn't need to glance over her shoulder to picture his progress. Every step he took made her chest cinch a little tighter.

"I want to stay here forever." Julianna's words rang as sweet as a prayer. "I don't want to be selfish like my mom, but I can't help it. It's one of the things I want real bad. A new mom is another."

"Oh, sweetheart." The snap of a twig behind her, and the pad of Adam's gait in the grass told her he was closing in.

"Are you finding any wild beasts?" His tone sounded light, but she could hear the strain behind his words.

He must have overheard his daughter's confession. Cheyenne ached for him, knowing full well the pain of a fractured family. She wished she could help, but caring and supporting were the best she could do. Also letting him and his girls know they weren't alone. She squared her shoulders, determined to make a difference.

"We haven't found anything dangerous yet, but that's a good thing." She matched his smile and rose from the side of the rippling stream. "A bear showing up would interrupt our party. It has before."

"I guess being swarmed by bees is a dull occurrence by comparison." He shrugged, holding the first-aid kit and a small bottle of calamine lotion. "At least no one was allergic."

"And only two of us got stung." She shook her head, scattering her auburn locks. "The view is worth the ride, don't you think?"

"I haven't seen anything like it." He held out his free hand as Julianna stepped over rocks and moss toward him. "Are we still on your land?"

"Yes. We own one of the biggest spreads in the county." She shrugged, as if the marvel of this place was no big deal. She'd grown up here where the sky was intensely blue and stretched forever above a patchwork of endless fields. He was blown away by those vibrant fields rimmed by craggy, breathtaking mountains that gave you the feeling God had reached down from heaven just to carve them.

"I don't see another soul out there. Other than the cattle and horses in that field." *Keep the conversation casual,* he told himself. His guard might still be mostly up, but he was struggling. The woman was tough on his defenses. Julianna's confession troubled him and he didn't want to admit it or, worse, have Cheyenne guess. He turned away abruptly out of self-protection and picked his way from beneath the shady trees and into the sun-swept meadow.

"We are spoiled here." Cheyenne seemed to think he was being complimentary.

He decided not to correct her. It was a strange feeling being surrounded by wilderness, by forest on one side and the long stretch of fields below. It reminded him how small he was, that all humans were. Similar to being up in an airplane and seeing with your own eyes how vast the world was from a new perspective.

"When I feel lost, I ride up here. It's easier to believe when you are in a place like this, surrounded by God's country. His Hand is everywhere. You can't miss it." She picked her way through wildflowers and grasses, keeping up with him. Her fingertips brushed his forearm, a show of kindness and an act of comfort. One he did not want, but her touch remained. *"Things always work out the way they are meant to. And we know that all things work together for good to those who love God."*

"Sure. One of my favorites." He could hear the coolness in his voice, although he did not mean it. When he pulled away from her touch, it was too quick, abrupt and a little panicked. He watched the dismay trail across her lovely face and the pinch of hurt settle around her eyes. The skin on his arm where her fingers were tingled like a dying nerve, sending shoots of painful prickles into muscle and bone. Even Julianna looked up at him reproachfully.

He was disappointed in himself, but he couldn't stop. The walls had to stay up. Panic rattled through him. Even trusting another woman who was no threat to him was too much. He wasn't ready for it. He doubted he would ever be.

"Come on, Julianna." He curled his fingers more tightly around her little hand. "I have things to do."

He winced at the confusion written across the child's button face. He grimaced harder at the upset darkening Cheyenne's eyes. She didn't deserve that, but he didn't know how to explain or apologize. Not one single word came to mind, his cerebral cortex had completely shut down. So in silence he turned away and led his daughter by the hand, leaving the woman behind in the meadow with daisies nodding at her feet and birds serenading her.

The shadows within him deepened until his entire spirit felt lost in darkness. He couldn't shake the feeling he had failed at something important, something that God had been hoping for. Disappointed in himself, Adam kept going. He did not look back.

* * *

"Tell me why Dad invited Adam?" Cheyenne asked her younger sister as she carried bags of marshmallows from the pantry and plopped them on the kitchen counter.

"It was Cady's idea." Addy piled chocolate bars onto the counter. "They are like family to her, you know. She thought the girls would get a kick out of the trail ride."

That didn't explain Adam's presence. He could have stayed at home, she thought, shaking her head. The man really bugged her.

"Those girls were so cute." Autumn gathered up a family-size graham cracker box. "Did you see how excited Julianna got when she saw the twin fawns hidden in the underbrush?"

"Beyond adorable," Rori added as she picked at the wrapping on a new roll of paper towels, trying to get it to open. "She wanted to go rescue them."

"It took a lot of convincing before she believed that their mom had left them there on purpose and we shouldn't interfere." Cheyenne yanked out the last bag and closed the pantry door. "Julianna worried about them all the way home."

"And all through the barbecue." Sierra sauntered over, skewers in hand. "My son finally made her understand that's the way fawns are raised, to stay where their mother tells them, but I'm not sure she completely bought it."

"Owen looked like he had a good time on the ride back with Dad." Definitely time to change subject. She hugged up the squishy bags of marshmallows into her arms. Their powdery scent permeated the plastic with a whiff of sugary goodness. "Did you see how Dad gave him control of Rogue's reins?"

"Yes, my little boy chattered about it nonstop for the entire two miles." Sierra's laughter rang carefree and light, proof of her happiness. Her wedding to Tucker was getting closer and closer. "Jenny was quiet, though. I hope getting stung on the arm didn't ruin things for her."

"No, she can be very quiet," Cheyenne spoke up, slightly miffed that the conversation had boomeranged back around to the new doctor. "It wasn't a serious sting and Adam took care of. It didn't seem to bother her during supper."

"I agree. It's totally handy having a doc around." Autumn headed to the back door. "Cheyenne, I saw you and him talking. Don't you think he's a nice guy?"

"Not so nice." She tried not to hold his abruptness against him or the fact that he hadn't glanced in her direction once—not *once*—as the afternoon turned to evening. She had just been trying to be friendly on the ride. A mistake, apparently.

"Really? I'll admit he's a little quiet." The skewers clinked and clanked as Sierra crossed the kitchen. "But he's a really good father. That's says everything about him."

"Not everything." Cheyenne rolled her eyes. "Can we please drop it? I'm not exactly a fan right now."

"I think she protests too much." Rori unwound the wrap from the paper towel roll.

"Ooh, I do, too," Addy agreed enthusiastically. "You don't think that means she likes him, do you?"

"I shouldn't have said a thing." She knew better, too. She had no one to blame but herself. If she had kept quiet, then the subject may have turned to something much more interesting by now.

"Maybe you are finally over Edward. Why not set your sights on the handsome doctor?" Autumn appeared hopeful as she gave the outside door a shove.

"He *is* handsome," Sierra agreed. "Not my type, obviously, since I'm about to marry Tucker. It's a purely objective observation."

"I agree. Adam is not as handsome as my Justin, but still, wow." Rori winked and sailed off to join the others.

Cheyenne covered her face with her hands. Seriously, if she said another word about Adam either way, they would never stop.

"Those girls of his are awfully sweet," Autumn's voice trailed after her, echoing in the kitchen. "I would take them in an instant."

"Who wouldn't?" Sierra agreed.

"Don't worry." Addy sidled closer. "I can distract them by mentioning Dad and Cady's big kiss in front of us. Do you want me to?"

"I'll survive." Her sisters could comment, quip and try to matchmake all they wanted. Adam wasn't interested any more than she was.

Especially after she overstepped her bounds. Twice. Talking marriage with him and then practically preaching to him. No wonder he'd been avoiding her. If she were in his shoes, she would, too, she thought, the last to leave the kitchen. She'd only been trying to be helpful, but she'd probably scared him good. When she bounded across the porch, his back was squared to her. Everyone was on the shady lawn, where flames leaped in the fire pit and conversations droned pleasantly.

"Cheyenne, I made this for you." Julianna's sweet voice startled her. The girl bopped off the porch swing and hopped to her feet. She held out a dandelion bracelet.

"Oh, it's lovely." What a sweet girl. She set

down the slippery marshmallow bags on the swing's wide cushion before holding out her right wrist.

"I have one, too." Julianna worked to secure the ends of the bracelet, twisting the stems. Her pigtails swung back and forth, as cute as could be. "Jenny and I made them all to match."

"You did a great job." Warmth filled her up, leaving little room to breathe. She and Julianna were kindred spirits, there wasn't a shred of doubt about that. She held out her arm to admire her new piece of jewelry. "Now we definitely match."

"We're the same." Julianna nodded in agreement, sparkling like the precious gem she was. "I can carry some of the marshmallows."

"That would be a great help, as I was in danger of dropping them." She handed the girl two bags to carry and took the other three.

"That's a lot of marshmallows." Julianna skipped down the steps.

"True, but with this family you can never tell how many marshmallows we are going to need. We believe in putting a lot of marshmallows in our s'mores."

"I like lots of chocolate."

"I won't hold that against you."

"Maybe I'll try lots of marshmallows *and* lots of chocolate."

"Sounds like a good plan to me. Maybe I will, too."

"Okay!" Julianna pranced across the grass. "Jenny! Look at all the marshmallows."

Someone was really excited. Cheyenne trudged after her, enchanted. The girl was a cutie, all bounce and sweetness as her sandals barely touched the ground.

"Julianna, look at how high the flames are." Jenny took a bag from her sister to help with the carrying. "It's a real bonfire like in the movies."

"We could signal planes with those flames," Dad quipped as he added the last of the folding lawn chairs to the circle around the campfire. "You girls sit down and get comfy. I don't suppose you kids want any s'mores. That's all right. That means there'll be more for me."

"No way!" Little Owen hurried up, hefting a folded chair all by himself. When the family was together, he was never far from Dad. "I got lots of room for s'mores."

"Me, too." Julianna hopped in place. "I'm real hungry."

"Then I sure hope there's enough for you kids because I'm hungrier." Dad winked and knelt to help Owen set up the chair the little boy was struggling with. Watching the big man and the small child working together made her smile. Owen would be Dad's first grandchild, and the bond between them was already strong. It was heartening to see.

She felt a prickle at the back of her neck. The sensation intensified as she dropped the marshmallows on the picnic table. She could practically feel every step Adam took toward her. He drained the oxygen from the air and the light from the sky. He brought the shadows with him as he towered over her, his gaze shuttered, as stoic as a rock.

"Daddy!" Julianna bounded up to him and grabbed his much larger hand with both of hers. "Frank said we get sparklers when it gets dark! Sparklers are my favorite."

"Yes, I'm aware of that." He sounded clipped and formal, but his dark gaze gentled when he gazed down at his youngest daughter.

"I love it here so much," Julianna gushed, caught up in the happy moment. "This is the best day ever."

"I'm glad, sweetheart." He tugged affectionately on one of her pigtails. "You're missing out on the s'more making."

"I am?" Her eyes popped wide as she flung around, startled to see Owen and Jenny at the picnic table with Dad. "Oh, no! Gotta go."

Cheyenne watched the girl dash away in a flash of purple. "She is revved up."

"Too much sugar and excitement, and it's apparently not over yet." Adam's dry sense of humor kept the darkness in his words from holding any bite.

"Not even close." Uncomfortable. She wasn't sure what a gal should say to a man who had made it clear she'd gotten too personal. Where were her sisters when a girl needed them? They were always hanging around, but when she was sputtering and in distress they were all huddled on the other side of the campfire chatting about Rori's pregnancy. Not that she wasn't interested, but how did she politely excuse herself from Adam and escape without making matters worse? Because no doubt it would be a very long summer dealing with him if she didn't.

He jammed his hands into his front pockets and stared deliberately away from her, as if to put more distance between them. His gaze remained glued on his daughters at the picnic table skewering marshmallows and offering their advice on s'more making to Owen.

Awkward. She slid her thumbs into her jeans pockets and gathered up the gumption to fix the problem she had made. It wasn't as if she and Adam could suffer like this through the next two months. "I shouldn't have asked about you remarrying. It was too personal. I wasn't hinting."

"I didn't think you were." Mountains could take lessons in inscrutability from the man. What was he thinking? It was impossible to tell with his dark glasses hiding his eyes and his mouth a thin, hard line.

"Or preaching at you. Sometimes in my eagerness to help, I go overboard. I see a problem and I can't help wanting to fix it, even if it's not my business."

"I understand." Not a single hint of emotion rang in his voice. He seemed fixated on the girls.

Maybe it would be better for both of them if she turned around, walked away and never so much as said hello to the man again. Yes, that sounded like the best plan. She spun around, her first step taking her in the direction of her sisters. The perfect refuge, especially since they were on the far side of the campfire, as far away from Adam as she could get.

"I didn't realize how well you knew my daughters." He broke the silence between them, calling her back.

She froze in midstep. She lowered her foot

to the spongy grass, feeling the cold arrow of his gaze pinned between her shoulder blades. Her escape thwarted, she swallowed hard, straightened her spine and tried not to notice how striking he was with the softer light of approaching sunset casting him in silhouette.

"We've spent some time together. Your daughters are easy to like."

"My girls must feel the same way about you."

"That doesn't sound like a compliment exactly." She squinted up at him, awash in sepia light. "Something about your tone. You haven't forgiven me for the marriage comment."

"I've forgotten about the marriage comment."

"It's a reasonable reaction. I get nervous when I talk about it, too. Who needs that kind of doom?" She tossed a lock of auburn hair over her shoulder, probably the prettiest woman he'd ever set eyes on and one of the kindest.

"I agree. It's taken me a while, but I've learned to avoid doom at all costs." The quip surprised him, rolling off his tongue when the last thing he wanted to do was let her close again.

"That's the reason for your dour demeanor. I get it." The fire danced behind her, tossing whimsical light to reflect the copper shades in her hair and outlining her with a gentle haze, as if heaven were drawing his attention directly to her. She was as stunning as a fairy-tale princess, wrapped in light and brightness and charm. She turned on her heel, walking away from him and said, "You don't have to be that way around me. You're perfectly safe."

"I don't believe that for a second." As her gaze caught his one last time, a frisson of awareness filtered through him, as gentle as the first hues of sunset, as sweet as the air he breathed. "You look like a walking hazard to me, drawing in everyone in your wake."

"Not true." She turned to walk backward, neatly skirting the fire pit. "I took an oath to help where I can. Even with you."

"Yes, that's what I meant."

It took a moment for her to realize the meaning of his compliment. Her smile turned dazzling. Its impact stealing the air from his lungs. Completely unaware of how she affected him, she spun around, called out a greeting to Buttercup, who mooed for attention at the fence. The cow watched Cheyenne with clear longing as the woman stopped to stroke her nose, gazing up at her lovingly.

At least his shields were up and full force once more, so it was safe to watch the woman from afar. The same warmth and care she felt for animals she showed toward people, and that warmth was what scared him. Life was easier existing in the shadows, where it was safe. He didn't know how Cheyenne had done it, but he was no longer in the darkness.

Chapter Seven

Cheyenne tucked the cell between her ear and her shoulder, waved goodbye to her boss and took the plastic hamster carrier from Ivy. Behind the clear Plexiglas, Tomasina cocked her head, watching her surroundings change as Cheyenne headed out the clinic's back door. Heat hit her like a steamroller. "Eloise, you've been on my mind today. I've been meaning to call."

"Busy day?" one of her best friends asked, sounding happy as always since she'd become engaged to Sean.

"*Busy* doesn't begin to describe it. *Hectic* or *insane* would be more accurate." She let the door swoosh shut behind her and headed straight to her pickup sitting in the dappled shade of a broadleaf maple. "This is the first sane minute I've had since I walked into the clinic. Not that I mind."

"Yes, I notice the note of joy in your voice. Would you be up for dinner tonight? I know it is last minute."

"Way too last minute." Which was a bummer. She set Tomasina's cage down in the shady flower bed instead of on the hot pavement, opened the door and swung into the seat. Blistering heat melted her as she started the engine, turned the AC on high and dropped her bag on the floor. "I already have plans. I'm returning Julianna's rescued bird to the wild. I'm not sure how long that is going to take."

"I would offer to wait and meet you when you're done, but I have a feeling you don't want to rush that visit."

"Why wouldn't I?" She hopped back out to retrieve the bird.

"Do you really think nobody noticed you and Adam getting along on the trail ride?"

"Sure, which means everyone would have noticed we *didn't* get along." At least she'd managed to sort of smooth things over with him. She knelt in front of Tomasina's cage. "You did notice how he went out of his way to keep his distance during the s'more making, right? And when the kids were running around with the sparklers?"

"Not really. I was a little absorbed." Eloise didn't sound ashamed of that one bit.

"Sean, I know." She rolled her eyes, thinking of how inseparable her cousin and her best friend had become. Sean and Eloise deserved great happiness and she wanted that for them. "You two were pretty snuggly around the campfire. Have you set a date yet?"

"We're thinking maybe an early-spring wedding."

"Ooh, romantic." The baby's soft black eyes sparkled and the bird opened her beak, eager for attention. Too cute. Cheyenne seized the handle, gently lifted the bird and rose to her feet. "Your grandmother must be thrilled."

"Are you kidding? Gran has already hunted down the best dress shop, the best florist, et cetera, and negotiated prices like a seasoned professional. I'm her first grandchild to marry in a long, long while."

"It's nice she loves you so much." She missed her grandmother, who had passed on. She would forever remember her snickerdoodles and loving kindness. Her Gran had been an animal lover, too. "Does she have the invitations printed already?"

"No, but only because I made her promise I got to pick them out. Which reminds me. I'm going to need a maid of honor. I don't suppose you would be interested?"

"I guess you could twist my arm." Laughing,

Cheyenne set the carrier on the passenger seat and worked the seat belt through the handle to keep Tomasina safe during the drive. "I would love to. Ooh, this will be so fun. When do I get to help you pick out stuff?"

"We'll see what Gran hasn't done yet and go from there." Eloise laughed. It was good to hear her so happy after her car accident several years ago. She sounded whole, like the girl she used to be. "There's another reason I'm calling. Cady wanted me to schedule a Granger girls at the spa day, her treat."

"What?" Cheyenne closed the door as carefully as she could so as not to startle the finch and circled around to the driver's side. "You mean a free day of pampering at the inn's spa? That sounds so great. I love Cady."

"Who doesn't? Is there any chance Nate can give you a day off soon?"

"I'll ask him and see." Blessed cool air fanned from the vents. She let it waft over her face as she settled behind the wheel. "I'll text you when I know."

"Great, then I can contact everyone else. We figured you are the busiest, so we are going to schedule around you. Cady is really excited."

"I am, too." She put the truck in gear and backed out of the spot. They talked for a few more minutes and made plans to meet as Cheyenne navigated down the residential streets of town, slowing at the intersections, stopping for an elderly couple to cross the street, waving at everyone who looked up from their flower bed weeding, lawn mowing or porch sitting. When she disconnected, she was alone with Tomasina. The bird watched her with a curious expression, as if wondering what exciting and new thing was about to happen next.

"I'm glad this has all worked out well for you, little one." She smiled at the baby as she pulled into a driveway sandwiched between fields. She winced when she recognized the luxury sedan parked in the detached carport. Adam was home. She'd been hoping to be in and out before he left work.

Oh, well. She pulled to a stop at the end of the gravel drive, shut off the engine and lifted the small cage. Tomasina watched trustingly. "I can do this. It doesn't have to be awkward or weird. I'll smile a lot and try not to say anything else I might regret."

The bird blinked, perhaps in agreement and so Cheyenne opened the door. Wind whistled through wild grasses next to the driveway as they headed toward the house.

"Cheyenne!" Julianna's excited voice rang in the air, a screen door slammed open and feet pounded on wood. The little girl leaped into sight, flying down the porch steps, her pigtails sailing behind her as she ran. "You brought her! Hi, Tomasina, remember me?"

The bird blinked again.

"Oh, she's so cute." The girl dropped to her knees on the lawn and studied the fragile creature. "She's all healed up now. She doesn't hurt anymore, does she?"

"No, she is feeling fine." She offered the girl the carrier. "You did a good thing in saving her, Julianna."

"I didn't save her. You and God did." The girl clutched the cage carefully and peered in at the bird. Her button face and sweet concern made her twice as cute.

"God surely did. I just took care of her wounds." She was thankful the Lord had answered Julianna's prayer. As she often did in her work, she felt His quiet presence. "Shall we get her back to her nest? I'm sure she really misses her family."

"Hi, Cheyenne!" Jenny strolled into sight. "I asked our neighbor Mr. Plum if we could borrow his ladder, and he brought it over and everything."

"That's great since my tree climbing skills are rusty."

She felt his approach even before the screen door squeaked open and his shoes padded on the porch. The unfriendly drum of his steps prepared her for the granite man, his face set, his eyes unreadable and as distant as the horizon. His brows knit together, his face darkened and severe lines dug in around his frown.

"The girls did tell you I was coming?" she said with her foot on the bottom porch step. "Because you look like a man who didn't have any warning."

"No. I wasn't aware." He raked a hand through his dark fall of hair, tousling it. He probably didn't realize that only made him more handsome. "You girls could have told me."

"We were going to, but you just got home." Jenny glibly appeared at top of the steps. "Right, Julianna?"

"Yep. Look at Tomasina, Daddy." The littler girl lifted the carrier. "Isn't she sweet? She's all well and everything. God fixed her."

"So I see." The smallest hint of amusement softened the hard set of his features. "It was a good thing you girls did in rescuing her."

Both girls beamed up at him, their affection as bright as their smiles. Maybe some of the family's wounds were starting to heal, Cheyenne thought as she followed everyone across the tiny porch and into the house, which had once been a stable. The interior was polished wood, softly stuccoed white walls and big sunlit windows. Julianna's dolls were forgotten on the living-room area rug, frozen in the middle of a picnic scene that included snappy summer fashions and a bright pink convertible.

"You'll have to excuse the disorder." Adam tossed over one wide shoulder as he crossed the room. "The girls didn't pick up their toys. They were supposed to."

"I like a little disorder." Cheyenne wasn't fooled by his tone. She looked around at the comfortable furniture and caught a glimpse of a tidy kitchen. Not only did he work hard as a doctor, he had made a home for his daughters.

As she remembered how her father had done the same, her throat caught with emotion. Dad had put in long days in the barns and on the range but he was always there to listen to stories of the school day, help with homework, praise good grades and sympathize with childhood heartaches. As she crossed the room, she saw the same commitment in this home. Hard not to respect and admire Adam for the man he was, a man who did whatever it required to take care of those he loved.

Her feelings for him had changed. She didn't want to admit it, but they had.

"That's the tree. I know because we saw her fall out and everything." Julianna led the way out the back door, carrier in hand. She peered in at the chick to make sure the little one was faring okay. "She went plop right on the grass."

"We were eating ice cream on the patio," Jenny explained. "She chirped but her mom couldn't help her."

"That's when the hawk swooped in and scooped her up." Julianna held up the cage, presumably so the chick could see her tree. "Are you ready to go home, Tomasina? I always am when I'm done at the doctor's."

"I'll get the ladder." Adam ambled away, the rich tones of his words lingering. He crossed the few yards to the side of the house where a ladder leaned in the shade, drawing her gaze.

Why couldn't she look away from him? She had really strong willpower, too, and it had no effect. He wore a blue T-shirt and khaki cut-offs, looking like he'd walked off the glossy pages of a catalogue with the wind in his dark hair and his muscles rippling as he carried the ladder. Overhead, the mama bird fluttered, chirping sharply at them. She was so not happy to return to her nest and find it surrounded by humans. Hungry chicks called out, singing a noisy chorus.

"Cheyenne, look!" Julianna held up the carrier. "Tomasina's chirping, too. She remembers her mom."

"I'm sure she's missed her very much." Cheyenne ripped her gaze away from the man settling the ladder against the apple tree's scaly trunk. It wasn't her business how many muscles he had or how attractively they rippled in his strong arms. Did he work out?

"I know what that is like." Julianna sighed, sadness chasing the warmth from the moment. Jenny hung her head.

"Oh." She hadn't meant to dredge up painful memories. How did she apologize? Adam gave the ladder a shake to see if it would hold. Tension bunched along his jaw. Had his walls gone up? She felt the cool brush of his gaze before he turned away. She swallowed hard, determined to do the right thing. "I know what that's like, too. My mom left when I was about your age, Julianna."

"She did? Then you know." Julianna leaned close and held the cage so they could look in at the bird together. "I'm so glad Tomasina can be with her mom again."

"Me, too." Easy to read the girl's raw pain and the wish for her mother's return. "Did you want to say goodbye to her?"

"Yes." Julianna's voice thinned. Jenny quietly sidled up to her as the girls bowed their heads together. Whispers and hushed words didn't quite carry on the wind. She took a step back to give them a little privacy.

"I could use a little help." Adam ducked as a second bird soared out of the sky directly toward him. "The mom called in reinforcements."

"The dad's trying to protect his family." She ducked, too, watching the brightly colored finch swoop close with a squawk. "That was nearly a kamikaze mission. He almost hit you. Are you all right?"

"That beak looks sharp. It missed me, but what about the girls?"

"They will be fine." Cheyenne shaded her eyes with her hands, squinting against the bright sun. The daddy bird landed on a branch beside his mate. The two parents cheeped at them in scolding tones. She wished she knew a way to tell them not to worry as she grabbed hold of the ladder, slipped her foot onto the bottom rung and gave a gasp as the contraption shimmied.

"Let me hold that for you." Adam moved in, his capable hands curling around the wooden sides, his breath fanning her hair. She was close enough to see the stubble of his five-o'clock shadow and the caramel flecks in his brown irises.

Just as she'd been able to sense his pain and

shadows, she saw his heart beneath the barriers, tender and caring. He might think he could hide his real self from her, but he would be wrong. She lifted her foot off the ground and climbed up a few rungs, enjoying the companionable feel of working together with him. Nice.

"Okay, Tomasina." Julianna lifted the carrier. "Don't be afraid."

When Cheyenne lifted the lid, the baby rocked with anticipation. The feel of the breeze and the green smell of trees and grass must have been a welcome sensation, because the chick held out her wings and fluttered. Her little round eyes gleamed as her siblings chorused again in hungry, hopeful twitters.

"Let's get you home, little one." She scooped the creature gently into her palm, enclosed her fingers just enough to keep the finch from falling and climbed two rungs. Working to keep her balance, Cheyenne straightened. Good thing Adam had a sturdy hold on the ladder. She could sense his watchful presence and his hand curved around her ankle, holding her solid. While alarmed parents dived, the nest full of chicks opened their beaks wide. She deftly nudged Tomasina into place in the middle and ducked before the daddy finch could skim the crown of her head.

"He almost got you, but you were fast." Adam's words were low, layered with a tone she couldn't discern as he released her ankle, but he remained on the ground beside her, holding the ladder with one hand and catching her elbow with the other. She didn't need the solid band of his fingers gripping her arm, but his friendliness was welcome.

"It's not my first baby bird rescue mission," she explained with a hop to the ground.

"That doesn't surprise me." His gaze fastened on hers and her heart skip three beats.

Strange. She shrugged it off and backed off a few paces. Jenny sidled up to her. Julianna cuddled her other side. While Adam hefted the ladder and leaned it against the house, they watched the father finch light on a limb and tweet at them in warning. Mama perched on the side of her nest and checked over her little ones. Chicks twittered and their song could have been a welcome home to Tomasina, at least Cheyenne hoped so.

"Is she going to be okay?" Julianna snuggled closer. Worry thinned her voice. "Her mom still wants her, right?"

"Right." Recognizing the real issue, Cheyenne slipped one arm around the girl.

"Good, cuz everybody needs a mom."

"The mama bird looks pretty relieved to see

all her babies are back in the nest. She's feeding them. I think that's Tomasina crowding to the front."

"Her poor siblings. I know just what it's like to have a pushy sister." Jenny glanced down at the ground, her dark hair falling forward to screen both the half smile and the sadness on her face. Happy for Tomasina, sad for their lost mother.

"I know that special feeling, too." Cheyenne slid her other arm around the older girl. Caring crept in. She could not hold it back.

"You were right, Cheyenne." Adam approached, hands in his pockets, studying the chicks tweeting in hopes of their parents return. "I don't know as much about animals as I think."

"Sometimes I think that's all I know." She unwound herself from the girls and knelt to take the carrier Julianna still clutched. "I'm a total animal person. Not so good with people."

"I don't know about that. You seem to be plenty popular around here." He nodded toward the girls.

"You're not leaving yet, are you?" Jenny asked, crestfallen.

"Don't go, Cheyenne." Julianna clutched the woman's hand, holding on with all her strength and pleading with all the might in her heart. "You have to stay for supper. We're havin' hamburgers."

"I made chocolate pudding for dessert." Jenny's forehead furrowed, her hands steepled and he could feel the girl's pull of want from where he stood.

"Maybe Cheyenne has plans." At least he hoped she did. This invitation wasn't something his daughters had cleared with him first. He fisted his hands, determined not to automatically shore up his defenses. He recognized the sympathy gentling Cheyenne's lovely features and her manner was equally as tender as she knelt until she was eye level with Julianna.

"My family expects me home." To her credit Cheyenne didn't look panicked at the idea of spending the evening in close proximity to him.

"Maybe you could call and ask permission." Julianna turned on the Bambi look. He knew exactly how hard that was to say no to. "If your dad says yes, then you can stay. That's what I do when I want to stay at a friend's. Back in New York, since I don't have any friends here. Yet. Except for Dusty. She's my best friend."

"My horse, Wildflower, has always been one of my best friends. Horses make great BFFs."

"You could be my best friend forever, too," Julianna offered.

He felt something break inside him. Not the walls surrounding his heart, but something more dangerous. The reserve he'd wrapped all the feelings he'd buried since Stacy admitted her affair was in danger of shattering. He'd been walking around like a half zombie, barely awake, simply existing. Like a dike crumbling, his emotions rushed upward with enough force that he could not hold them back.

His daughters were still hurting. Standing in the dappled shade surrounded by green grass and blue sky and with the world alive and vibrant around them, they were as caught in shadow as he'd been. He'd tried hard to steer everyone onto a sensible path, to keep life as solid and practical as possible that he hadn't been able to measure the true problem. He had to admit that not wanting to examine his feelings made it harder for him to recognize and help them with theirs. What kind of father did that make him?

"I would love being friends with you, with both of you." Cheyenne could see what he had not. Her tenderness toward the girls, her care with their feelings, her sincere offer of friendship made his chest cinch so tight it hurt to breathe. She wasn't just a good vet but a truly caring woman. "I think we are already birds of a feather."

"Uh," Jenny groaned at the pun, hiding her laugh.

"Then you have to stay. Friends eat over at each other's houses all the time." Julianna looked so vulnerable with the depth of her heart shining in her eyes. It was all he could do not to scoop her up and hold her tight, to find a way to give her what she'd been missing, what he hadn't even realized he'd been denying her.

"I'll give my dad a call." Cheyenne reached into her pocket and pulled out her bright pink phone. Every little movement she made was graceful as if timed to music, and his spirit responded like she was a song his soul already knew.

Chapter Eight

"Jenny, this is good pudding." Cheyenne let the creamy chocolaty goodness glide over her tongue. "You did a really good job."

"It was just the instant kind." Jenny shrugged and dug her spoon into the bowl on the patio table in front of her, dismissing the compliment as if it didn't much matter. Her tiny smile said it did.

"Chocolate's my favorite." Julianna licked her spoon.

"Me, too." Cheyenne smiled and dug her spoon into her bowl for another bite.

"We're like twins." Julianna gazed up at her with those big Bambi eyes and leaned her head against Cheyenne's arm.

"Twins except for I'm a lot taller than you," she couldn't help teasing.

"And your hair is reddish and mine's brown."

"Exactly." Funny. Warmth whispered through her, cotton-candy sweet.

"Chocolate is my favorite, too." Jenny swirled her pudding into a swirly mountain peak. "Does that mean we're triplets?"

"Triplets at heart." Cheyenne couldn't escape Adam's scrutiny. He watched her in the same way he'd been watching her since she'd returned Tomasina to her nest. No longer dour, but a furrow had dug into his forehead and stayed there throughout the meal, which he'd barbecued on the patio. He'd listened to the females talk about birds, horses, how they were progressing with the riding lessons Autumn was giving them in her spare time and he'd hardly commented. She sensed something had changed, but she didn't know what. Who knew what the man was thinking?

It was to remain a mystery because he pushed back his chair, gathered his empty bowl and rose from the table. Dappled shade from the long shadows sifted over him as he hesitated. A pleasant softness settled within her as he studied her silently. Her guard fell down; perhaps it was because she was full from a tasty meal, had spent time being charmed by the Stone girls, and then there were the effects of the sugary chocolaty pudding. Must be bliss overload, she told herself, feeling something strange and unfamiliar stirring within her, a sensation she'd never felt before.

Definitely chocolate overload, she decided. Best to stick with the safest explanation. But was it the truth? She didn't know. Time froze and the single moment when Adam's gaze met hers stretched into an eternity. Her pulse stilled, her breathing stopped, she could see nothing but him towering above her, the lazy breeze ruffling the ends of his hair. So vibrant and strong and real she could not look away.

His gaze pierced her, as if he could see all the way to her soul. She didn't have the barriers to stop him. She didn't know where they had gone, but she felt exposed to him, as if he could see the scars in her spirit and the disillusion she didn't know if she could overcome.

She might insist she was over what's-his-name, but that was sheer stubbornness and wishful thinking. Was that what Adam could see? She didn't know because he broke away to take his empty dish into the kitchen. The connection between them snapped, her pulse kick-started, time marched forward and he turned away. The noise, color, scents of the world returned. She sat blinking in the chair with the rush of sound ringing too loud in her ears and the brightness of the evening stinging her eyes.

"Cheyenne, now that we're friends we can

go riding and stuff, right?" Julianna looked up, still leaning against her arm, her soulful gaze framed by innocent curly lashes and tufts of brown hair that had escaped from her scrunchies.

"Yeah." Jenny dug her spoon into the pudding mountain she made and took a small bite. "We're starting to get really good. You saw us on the trail ride. Maybe we could do that again?"

"Maybe not the same trail ride, since that takes an entire afternoon." She mentally flipped through her calendar—work, a weekend on call, upcoming wedding prep, not to mention the ranch work she'd volunteered for. "I'm sure we can fit in another trail ride sometime."

"Yay!" Julianna bounced in her chair. "How about now?"

"The horses are at Cady's stables," Jenny stated practically, sitting tall, in charge. She looked down her nose at her little sister. "Wildflower is on the Granger ranch. We can't ride tonight. It's not set up."

"Tomorrow?" Julianna was not easily defeated.

"Tomorrow I have dinner plans with Eloise."

"What about the weekend?" Jenny asked.

"I have a final dress fitting in Jackson on

Saturday and I'm probably helping with the haying on Sunday."

"Oh." Both girls deflated.

"How about after Sierra and Tucker's wedding? I'm sure I will have time then."

"We'll talk Dad into it." Julianna's earnestness was priceless. "I know he'll say yes."

"You do?" Baritone rumbled like thunder. The screen door creaked and Adam ambled onto the patio.

"I just have a feeling, Dad." Julianna beamed up at him.

"That I can't say no to you?" He tugged on a pigtail gently. "Don't count on it. I've decided to institute a new policy in this house. The answer is no from now on."

"You aren't fooling us." Jenny scooped a last bite from her bowl, her forehead furrowing as if in deep thought. "Maybe you should come, too. Now that you know how to ride and everything."

"Yeah, Dad!" Julianna jumped to her feet, clasped her hands together and turned on the charm. "Please, please, please?"

"I've done about all the horse riding I can take." Get up on another horse? Just because last time had gone well and without incident didn't mean it would again. "I'll cheer from the sidelines."

"We're going on a ride, Dad, not around the corral." Jenny dropped her spoon in her bowl and reached across the table to take charge of Cheyenne's and Julianna's empty bowls. "You could walk along with us, but it would be embarrassing."

"Yes, people will talk," Cheyenne chimed in sweetly. She knew his secret. He never should have revealed the details of the mean horse incident. "Word like that gets around, your reputation as a doctor will suffer. This is horse and cattle country."

"I'm not afraid of a little gossip."

Her gaze collided with his. Why did he feel as if he were falling into that mischievous blue?

"I'm just thinking of your girls. Having a father walking instead of riding would be a tough humiliation for them to endure."

"So you will have to come along, Dad." Jenny smiled secretly at her sister as if they had some ulterior motive.

"How did I get roped into this, I don't know." He stood and took the pile of bowls from Jenny. "You girls go play."

"That means yes." Julianna shouted over her shoulder on her way to a swing set tucked in the far corner of the lawn. "Look, Tomasina is still in her nest. At least she's not on the ground."

"Thanks, Dad." Jenny's tone held meaning

beyond her words, a meaning that tugged at him, pulling him in a direction he didn't want to go.

He'd agreed to a summer here but his children wanted more. They had horses they had grown close to, new adventures like trail riding and Granger barbecues. The summer was ticking away. July would be gone before they knew it and once they reached the last week in August, they would be packing up for their old life. A life they no longer wanted, but he did.

"Let me take those in." Cheyenne's alto broke apart his thoughts.

He'd forgotten he was holding the bowls. "No, you're a guest. I'll take care of these. I have some sweet tea made if you're interested."

"Perfect." She rose from the chair, trailing him across the patio. "I wouldn't have pegged you for a sweet tea drinker."

"Does that mean you take me for a sour kind of guy?" He held the screen door for her, inhaling the faint scent of vanilla. Her hair rippled like cinnamon silk as she waltzed by.

"If the shoe fits."

"I deserved that." He followed her into the kitchen, glancing toward one of the windows to keep watch. Julianna was on the swing, while Jenny fished her cell out of her pocket and began to text. He plunked the bowls into the sink. "I wasn't in the best mood when you arrived."

"So I noticed. It couldn't have been a long workday here, could it?"

"It was. I had two new patients from neighboring towns. Business is picking up." He grabbed two plastic glasses from a cupboard and headed to the fridge. "Stacy called right before you came. She isn't happy I brought the girls out here. Our conversation didn't go so well, but I think when she spoke to the girls it went better."

"I thought I noticed a little extra sadness when we were talking about moms."

"She walked out on us. She demanded a divorce. I'm hoping in time it won't be as acutely traumatic for the girls." He grabbed the pitcher, fighting the urge to close up entirely and it wasn't easy. He'd been dealing with life that way for so long. Closed up, he couldn't feel anything. Closed up, he didn't risk letting anyone see how inadequate he felt. "It always takes me a while to calm down after I talk to her."

"Sorry I had such bad timing. I should have chosen another night to bring Tomasina."

"No. The girls had a better evening because you came by." He replaced the pitcher and closed the refrigerator door. "They are doing better and better every day they are here."

"That's the effect of Wyoming's wide-open spaces. Life is good here."

"I would have argued with you a few weeks ago, but not today." He felt at ease with her. Just the two of them in the kitchen and not a hint of panic. Whatever initial response he'd had to her had transformed into an ultra sense of calm. Maybe because he knew he had nothing to worry about with her. The way she treated his children, every animal she came across and the care she'd shown the baby bird revealed the real Cheyenne Granger. "I didn't want to move out here. I wanted to stay in New York. I miss New York."

"Sure, but this country is growing on you." She wrapped her long, slender fingers around one glass. Healing hands, gentle hands. A woman who made what difference she could in the world.

He caught a glimpse of his old self, the Adam Stone he'd once been. It was easier to believe he could be that man again as he took his tea and held the door for Cheyenne.

"I admit it. I like a few things about life in this town." The fresh air was one of them, redolent with grass and rose fragrance from the flower beds and a general green smell that he would never forget. Years in the future, back home going through paperwork in his office he would remember the scent of the Wyoming breeze and this evening when his children were laughing and he felt safe and relaxed.

"You like a few things. Really? That many?" She twinkled at him, sparkling from the inside out. She settled into the chair next to him, tall and willowy and elegant in her country-girl way. "Name one."

"I like the ice cream down at the drive-in."

"They make it by hand." She took a sip of tea. "Ooh, this is good. What else?"

"There is no traffic congestion. No waiting in any line anywhere. Housing is cheaper. My girls are better here. They need this summer." He also realized a big truth about himself. "I do, too."

She merely nodded, as if she understood the rest of what he could not say. It had been a long time since he felt he could trust a woman. Sure, he had Cady to turn to, but she was like family. With Cheyenne, it was different. He didn't know why. He took a sip of tea and let the sweetness sluice across his tongue. It was a pleasant evening. He could hear every sound the wind made through the tree leaves, through the grass blades and the faint tinkle of Mrs. Plum's wind chimes an acre away.

He didn't know what it was about Cheyenne, but he felt amazingly comfortable with her. Companionable. He glanced over to check on his daughters again—Jenny was sitting cross-legged in the grass, her thumbs flying over the keys, Julianna swung higher and higher, pigtails flying. He cleared his throat. "You've prodded and probed. Now it's my turn."

"What? I didn't prod. I didn't probe."

"With your questions you did." He almost chuckled. The small rumble rising in his chest seemed to break a piece of his emotional scar tissue, and he breathed easier. "Why is a woman like you still single?"

"Oh, you're wondering what exactly is wrong with me, is that it?" Amused, she studied him over her glass rim. A shadow darkened her but when he blinked, it was gone. "I am fully committed to staying single."

"Fully committed? That's a strong statement."

"Backed by a strong sentiment. Let's just say my last Valentine's Day was traumatic, and I'm now single and totally determined to stay that way." She shrugged as if nothing bothered her from that experience. From all appearances she was a woman too strong and confident to have been wounded by love.

He'd thought he was too strong and confident, too, and yet his failure to keep his wife and to make his marriage last had knocked him to his knees. He was a man used to success, he had triumphed at everything else he'd attempted in life. He wondered if Cheyenne might be similar, successful on so many levels but not when it came to what mattered most.

Her cell chose that moment to ring. Relief flashed across her face, a face lovelier every time he looked. She dug the phone from her trouser pocket and glanced at the screen. "Saved by the bell. I have to take this. It's work."

"I know all about being on call." He leaned back in his chair, listening to the clear notes of the birds singing and feeling a deeper peace roll through him. He watched her rise from her chair with ballerina grace and a sprinter's energy.

"This is Dr. Granger," she said into the phone, moving away toward the rail, intent on the call. She was serious about her work and capable, not at all the kind of woman he went for. Maybe that was why he was at ease with her. Maybe that explained why he could open up to her.

"Okay, Martha. I'll be right over." While she'd pitched her voice into the phone, the reassuring tones sailed to him on the evening breeze. "Stay calm. There's no reason to worry. Everything will be fine. I'll see you in five minutes, tops."

"Trouble?" He rose from the table, already knowing she had to go.

"Martha Wisener's very beloved prized cat is about to have kittens and she wants me there." Cheyenne tucked her phone into her pocket. She looked lovely enfolded in the soft, dappled shade. She was everything good, everything he'd stopped believing in. "Martha's just a tad nervous."

"No high risks, no complications?"

"No. I've known Martha all my life—how can I say no?" She shrugged as if she didn't mind at all, or perhaps she was glad to have an excuse to avoid his earlier question.

"Then you can spare one moment." He moved in front of her, blocking her escape. "I want to hear your answer."

"I can't imagine why."

"Neither can I." His smile stretched his face, the widest smile he'd had in too long to count. The stretch of his heart matched. "Tell me."

"It was typical, I guess. Every girl probably has this happen to her at one time or another." Her chin went up, her shoulders squared and hurt glittered in poignant blue. She blinked but the hurt remained. Casual, as if she were talking about the weather, she waved one hand as if it were no big deal. "I fell for Edward at vet school."

"So this was recent?"

"Fairly. We got along well together. I started imagining a future with him, but he was just going through the motions, biding his time. Edward wanted a girlfriend, but I wasn't The One. He knew it. I was convenient for him, nothing more. I figured it out eventually, but the damage was done."

"You left out a lot from that story." He didn't move from of her path. "The same way I left out a lot in the telling of mine."

"Then you can guess at what I didn't say."

"Yes." He swallowed, the low notes of his baritone dipping richly. "I'm sorry you went through that."

"A lesson I will never forget." She didn't mention Edward had been her first real love. Her one vulnerable, inexperienced romance and her heart was still badly bruised from it. She had been the studious girl in high school, too serious for the boys in her class. She wasn't exactly a social butterfly in college and still wasn't, since she felt more comfortable with animals than people. Edward had been exactly the kind of man she'd once dreamed of—smart, funny, kind and loved animals. It would have been better if she told Adam all of that, but what rolled off her tongue? The things she most wanted to keep secret.

"I shouldn't have expected so much." She had never caught a man's attention before, so perhaps that should have been a clue. She'd expected everything with Edward. Maybe she wasn't the kind of woman who instilled the need to love, cherish and protect in a man. Maybe there was some reason she wasn't lovable romantically.

"That's how I feel, too." Adam's confession surprised her. "We have a lot more in common than I first thought. I suppose I will see you again sometime?"

"In a town as small as this, that is a certainty." She tugged her truck keys from her pocket. She ignored the tingle of awareness when she skirted by him, whisper close, and attributed it to her emotional turmoil. Edward was not a pleasant memory.

"Cheyenne, are you leaving?" Jenny looked up from typing on her phone.

"Duty calls. Kittens are on their way into this world as we speak."

"Wait! Don't go yet." Julianna skidded to a stop on the swing and bounded across the lawn. "Can I come, too? I want to see kittens being born."

"Not this time, cutie. I'm sorry." Cheyenne was touched when the girl launched against her in a sweet hug. Fondness trickled in as she hugged the girl in return before stepping away. "How about I send you a picture after they are born, if Martha says it's okay?"

"Yes." Julianna bounced while Cheyenne handed over her phone to Jenny, who competently punched her number into the device. "I'm so excited. Dad, did you hear? Kittens. Do you think—"

"No." Adam cut her off with a wink and an easy grin that doubled his amazing masculine charisma. "No kittens this time, but maybe somewhere in the far and distant future."

"Oh, Daddy! You finally understand." Julianna clasped her hands, steepling them as if in prayer, transformed with a higher level of adoration for her father. "I want a kitten and a puppy and a horse and a cow like Buttercup."

"Stop. We can't fit all that into our house back home." He actually joked, the humor a definite improvement. Cheyenne couldn't hold back a little sigh. The man was striking enough to steal her heart.

If she was in the market, that is. Good thing she wasn't interested in romance with Adam or anyone. She took her phone from Jenny, said her goodbyes and headed down the walkway to her waiting truck. The sun brightened like a beacon but it could not be a sign.

She buckled up, started her engine and drove away.

Chapter Nine

"Yes, Sean and I have set a wedding date." Eloise squinted across the length of the cab of Cheyenne's truck to bring the drive-in's menu into focus. "We're looking at Valentine's Day. A little cliché, but it just seems to fit us."

"It's certainly perfect," Cheyenne agreed as she upped the air-conditioning now that her window was down. Hot, dry July air blasted in like a furnace. Sometimes love was right, you could look at a couple and see they had what it took to go the distance. It was as obvious with Eloise and Sean as the sky above. "The two of you make the best couple. Nothing could be sweeter than you two."

"Oh, stop. I'm just thankful to have found my happily ever after." Eloise folded a lock of blond hair behind her ear. "What about you?"

"Me and happily ever after? I can't see it happening anytime soon."

"Are you sure there isn't anyone who interests you at all? Even a little?"

"No, I'm drawing a blank." She couldn't think of a single eligible bachelor in these parts who held her interest in the least. "You know the saying, 'All the good ones are taken.'"

"Edward really hurt you, I know. But trust me when I say that the right man is out there somewhere for you, a man who won't let you down. If it happened for me, it can definitely happen for you."

"Not likely." The clump, clump of a waitress on roller skates brought an end to the exact subject Cheyenne didn't want to talk about. She'd hashed over her disastrous mistake with Edward enough lately. "Hey, Chloe, do you know why the diner was closed?"

"I'm totally clueless." The teenager flashed a bright smile as she skidded to an awkward stop. She caught the speaker for balance with one hand and pulled out her order pad with the other. "It was open for lunch, that's all I know. What can I get you two?"

After they gave their orders to Chloe and watched her thump away on her skates, Cheyenne deliberately turned the conversation away from any talk of bachelors, Edward or her unmarried state. "How are the rescued horses doing?"

"Thriving, which is nice to see after all that has happened to them. I'm glad Cady decided to fill the inn's stables with unwanted horses." Eloise unbuckled and leaned back in the seat, getting comfortable. Mischief glimmered in her eyes. "The Stone girls spend a lot of time there. Sad how their mom abandoned them. Their dad is real handsome, isn't he?"

"I would say passable."

"Hardly. He's got that tall, dark and serious thing going on. Besides, you've been spending *so* much time with him."

"Not intentionally. How did you know about last night?"

"Jenny and Julianna hung out with Cady at the inn this afternoon. I heard firsthand how you put Tomasina back into her nest and stayed to have supper with Adam."

"With his *family*," she corrected. "I'm friends with the girls, not with the father."

"But you spent a lot of time with him on the trail ride. I looked over my shoulder quite a few times to see the two of you talking like old friends."

"Only for part of the time and not like old friends. More like two strangers trying to have a polite conversation." A tight knot of emotion bunched behind her sternum, emotion she didn't want to feel. He'd opened up to her; she had been drawn to do the same and now she didn't know what to think. "I'm not sure why God has put him in my path."

"Maybe it will take time to find that out. I believe the Lord has good plans ahead for you."

"Sure, but it can't be for the reason you are imagining."

"Why wouldn't God have a great romance in store?" That's what being happily engaged did to a woman—it made her see romance everywhere.

"Because I'm avoiding relationships of the romantic variety, so a great romance is impossible. I refuse to let it happen." She paused to roll down the window. Chloe handed over two sodas and two big bags of food with good cheer. The fragrant greasy scent of hot French fries filled the cab as she skated away.

"If not romance, then why are you and Adam being put together? Go ahead, I'm listening." Eloise unrolled one of the bags.

"Everyone in town has heard how his wife left him." The bag crinkled as she extracted a red-checked French fry container and set it on the console. "My family went through the same thing long ago. I'm in a position to understand and maybe even help."

"The girls are hurting," Eloise agreed, her expression growing serious as she opened the glove box and used it as a tray for her basket of fries. "As happy as they are spending time with the horses and with Cady, the shadow is always there beneath the surface."

"Yes. I remember feeling that way. I could almost forget what had happened but never quite get beyond the fact Mom left." She extracted a straw from the bag and unwrapped it thoughtfully. She'd been doing a lot of thinking about this. Last night with Adam had been companionable and she felt, well, she didn't know what she felt. Her emotions were muddled and not easy to analyze—not that she wanted to. "Maybe God is calling me to help Julianna and Jenny. With the animals that Julianna has been finding who need my help, I have to wonder if God is at work, leading me where I am needed most."

"I would be disappointed if that were the only reason, at least for your sake. I want you to find the happiness I have." Eloise poked her straw into the plastic lid of her soda cup, her voice gentling with the understanding only a good friend could have. "But if you are being called to help those girls, then that is just what those sweet children need."

Relief slipped into her heart, refreshing as an

icy drink on a hot summer day. Eloise had said the precise words she needed to hear. The Lord had brought any number of souls in need into her life—albeit mostly animals. Julianna had to be a kindred soul for a reason. Cheyenne knew she was meant to help the girl and her sister, and that her heart with its scars would be kept safe.

"As for the whole romantic issue," she said in jest as she dug her cheeseburger out from the bottom of the sack, "I'm done with it. Going to skip it entirely. Maybe I should get a dog. They are great for companionship."

"They are, plus you can tell them what to do and they obey."

"Yes. Dogs are trainable. Men, not so much." With a smile, she crumpled up the sack. "Do you want to say grace?"

"I'd be happy to." Eloise smiled in return, another kindred spirit the Lord had blessed her with.

Adam cleaned the lint from the trap, listening to the muffled voices down the hall. The girls were speaking too low to make out the words, but they sounded cheerful about something they wrote with a sparkly pen. Their happiness was a nice change, considering their mother's call had come at a pivotal time when both the girls had hit a good stride, were settled in here and happy.

Lord, help this to get easier for them. The prayer accompanied the twist of the dial. He hit Start and as the dryer chugged to life, he tried to have confidence that interaction with Stacy would be better for the girls over time. He grabbed the full clothes basket, closed the small laundry room door behind him and followed the chime of little girl voices to their room at the end of the hall.

"Cheyenne," the girls said together with a cheerful trill of laughter. When he rapped his knuckles on the open door, both of them jumped and guilt dug into their button faces.

Guilt? He wondered what they were up to now. Probably planning another reason to ride those horses they'd fallen in love with at Cady's stable. He dropped the clothes basket on the foot of Julianna's twin bed. "Okay, what are you two troublemakers up to?"

"Nothing." Jenny's guileless innocence was suspect.

So was the mischief in Julianna's dark eyes. "We were just talkin'."

"So I heard." He began sorting socks, making a stack for Julianna's and one for Jenny's. "Would you like to clue me in?"

"No, we're fine, thank you." Julianna glittered a little more. "Daddy?"

He knew she couldn't keep quiet for long. He was about to discover the subject the girls had been conspiring about. "What?"

"We gotta have new stuff. Can we go shopping tomorrow?"

Not the Bambi eyes. He squared his shoulders, straightened his spine and steeled himself against the power of that gaze. "It seems to me you already have enough stuff."

Julianna's brow furrowed. She tilted her head to one side, considering her answer before she opened her cupid's mouth. "But we don't have the right stuff, Daddy. I need new books real bad."

"Books." That was the hardest thing for him to say no to, and he figured the girls knew it. He tossed a pink T-shirt on Julianna's clothes pile and a ruffled T on Jenny's. He didn't miss how they were both watching for the slightest hint he was wavering. "I've changed my mind. All that reading you do? It's bad for you. I think you should both stop."

"Dad!" Jenny rolled her eyes. "You are *so* not funny."

"Oh, I don't know about that. I'm grinning." He tossed a pair of summer pajamas with dogs printed on them on the Julianna stack, realizing he was grinning. How about that. Summering in Wyoming was doing him good. "What does Cheyenne have to do with your sudden need for books?"

"For horse books, Dad." Julianna shook her head sadly, as if she felt sorry for her poor, slow-witted father. "Cheyenne knows all the goods ones."

"She texted us a whole list." Jenny gave her phone keys a few taps. "There. She said she'll think up more titles and get back to us, and I said okay."

"You are bothering Cheyenne at this time of night?" It was nearly the girls' bedtime. "You two are going to wear out your welcome with her."

"We're friends." Julianna bounced off the edge of her bed and began to match up her socks. "Friends can text each other anytime. Dad?"

"What now?" He grabbed the last garments from the basket and tossed them onto their respective piles.

"I can't text because I don't have a phone. It would be real handy if I had one."

"I'm sure it would." He shook his head when Jenny's phone chimed. "Now get these clothes folded and put away, and then brush your teeth for bed."

"I want a pink phone, like Cheyenne's." Julianna rolled up a pair of socks, pigtails swinging as she worked.

"I'll keep that in mind." Why wasn't he surprised? The woman's image sluiced into his thoughts like the gentle waters of a creek, flowing lazily. Mental pictures of her leading the cows off the road, of the sympathy in her blue gaze when she'd realized how afraid he was of horses and of the compelling gentleness that made her beautiful and easy to trust.

He grabbed the empty basket and stepped out into the hall. The girls were huddled side by side over the phone, giggling excitedly over something on the screen. Something from Cheyenne.

The woman was treacherous. If he wasn't careful, he would fall for her and fall hard. That was the last thing he wanted to do, the one thing he was not ready for.

He headed down the hall, dropped the basket in the laundry room and stretched out on the couch, where a book awaited him. He wasn't aware that he was whistling the whole time.

That was one long day, and Frank Granger felt it in his bones. Dog tired, he gave Buttercup one last scratch behind the ears. The heifer, curled up on the soft lawn for the night, fluttered her long curly lashes at him.

"You have a good night, sweetheart." He checked the gate to make sure there would be no escaping down the driveway and clomped onto the porch. Moonlight lit the way to the back door. His muscles protested as he hunkered down on the bench in the mudroom to kick off his boots. His joints ached, his muscles protested and his work wasn't done yet. He would see the glory of an early dawn from the cab of his tractor tomorrow. He planned to get as much work as he could in before heading over to the tux shop in Jackson. The weather had stayed good for cutting, and this time of year it never lasted. Thunderstorms popped up but wet hay wasn't his top worry these days.

He hung his hat on a peg and wandered into the dark kitchen. The faint scent of meat loaf lingered in the air. Mrs. G. had left the kitchen spick-and-span and he grabbed a cold glass of milk and a handful of ginger snaps from the porcelain cow cookie jar, which had been his mother's.

The house echoed around him, as empty as could be. There used to be a time when so much noise filled this house it was deafening. A time when a baby was teething, toddlers were at play, his girls racing through the house playing ball or tag and his boys in the middle of a rough-and-tumble wrestling match.

He stopped in the family room, took a soothing swallow of milk and remembered. His chest ached a little with the power of those long-ago times. Of later years when the kids were busy with homework, after-school projects, teenage woes and the sadness when Lainie left.

He bit into a cookie, soft just the way he liked it, bless Mrs. G., and headed through the double doorway of his study. The room had always been his sanctuary during the rambunctious times. It was his hideaway to deal with bills and budgets and taxes and, if he wasn't in the mood for those things, to bury his nose in a ranching magazine.

These days his movements whispered around him, noisier in the vast stillness than the pleasant chaos of those lost days had ever been. For a long time he believed the best part of his life was behind him, but as he nudged a framed photo on his desk closer, he had to admit his life had taken a whole new turn. He polished off the cookie, let the chewy goodness fall onto his tongue and the silence shattered.

The back door squeaked open, footsteps drummed on the floor and the thump of boots being taken off and hitting the hardwood echoed through the family room. Sounded as if Cheyenne had found her way in from her late shift in the fields.

"Dad? Are you around?"

"In here." He nudged the photograph closer, a snapshot he'd taken about a month ago at Autumn's wedding. His heart tugged at the sight of his beautiful daughters surrounding Cady, who was in the middle of the group smiling at the camera as pretty as could be. Cady. That woman had stolen him, heart and soul.

"Addy says she'll be driving in early in the morning. She's tired, so she's stopping for the night. She'll make it for the final fitting." She called out to him and the patter of her gait grew closer, accented by the faint tap of keys and an electronic chime. Cheyenne rounded the corner, more chipper than he'd seen her lately. Something had put a snap in her step.

"That's sensible of her. Type howdy from me." He swiveled his chair around. Just yesterday Cheyenne was a little auburn-haired sprite trailing him through the barn at his knee, doctoring cow and horse alike with her earnest sympathy. He thought of all the hours they'd put in together nursing a calf with pneumonia back from the brink, bringing a new foal into the world or staying up all night with a colicky horse. He could still see the glimpse of his little girl in the woman with her hair pulled into a ponytail, wearing an old feed-store T-shirt and battered jeans.

"There. Message sent." She went to pocket her phone but another chime stopped her. "Oh, not from Addy. It's from Jenny."

"Jenny Stone?"

"Yes, I recommended some horse novels I thought she and Julianna might like. They are big readers." Her smile widened as she typed a response. Something within her brightened more.

Interesting.

"They are meeting with me at the bookstore in Jackson tomorrow. I figure I can squeeze that in before the dress fitting." She glanced up enough to reveal the dazzle lighting her eyes. "You know how I love a good horse story."

"Sure." He doubted that was the reason the girl glowed from the inside out. "You're awfully taken with those girls."

"We have a lot in common." She finished typing and slipped the phone into her jeans pocket. "There. Done. How about you? Did you and Justin make good progress in the south forty?"

"We got all of it cut. A big job, too, what with having to take part of tomorrow off." Nerves bunched in his chest like a heart attack, but he faced the fear head-on. "I was wondering what you girls were up to before your appointment at that fancy bride shop."

"We were going to meet for lunch at our favorite burger place. It's been a while since we all sat down together. This summer has been crazy and it's not over yet." She leaned against the door frame. "Why? Did you need me to run an errand for you?"

"Not exactly." Sweat broke out all over, collecting on his palms, beading on his forehead, snaking down the back of his neck. The nerves began to press with the weight of an elephant. He'd made up his mind, so he couldn't let a bucket load of panic stop him. "I need you girls to meet me sometime before or after your dress appointment."

"Sure. What is it? You don't have bad news, do you? You don't look well suddenly. Really pale." She launched off the doorjamb to kneel at his feet. "Correct that. You're totally ashen. Are you having any chest pain?"

"Don't worry, missy." He chuckled. If he didn't know better, he would worry about the stymieing pain in his chest, too, but it was purely emotional. "I need help picking out an engagement ring. I don't know where to start."

"*What?*" Surprise passed across her darling face. Her eyes widened with delight. A smile cinched up her mouth in sheer glee. "Oh, Dad! You're going to propose to Cady."

"Shh, now that's a secret between you and me, at least until tomorrow. Will you set it up for me?"

"I got my phone. It'll take a few text messages and we're set." She flung her arms around him and he gave himself permission to hold on tight, just for one too-short moment. All the years behind him, valuable beyond belief, came back around again. It was like holding the little girl his Cheyenne used to be. Too soon she broke away, ecstatic, his beloved daughter. Her ponytail bounced as she fished her phone out of her pocket.

"Daddy, this is great. We all love Cady so much. Oh, I'm going to burst not being able to tell anyone. Don't wait very long to ask her or I won't be able to stand it." Her blue eyes shone with a deep joy he hadn't expected. Her thumbs stilled on the little keyboard of her phone. "It's time you found some happiness of your own. You worked hard to raise us and you never faltered. You deserve this, Dad."

"I don't know about that, but I won't say no to it." He'd learned one thing. Life is shorter and love is more precious than you think. Time rolls on by with no way to slow it down. Babies turn into children; in a blink they become adults, and your life is half-spent. He was going to take this opportunity the Lord had brought him and enjoy every minute, because those minutes just kept passing.

Chapter Ten

"Cheyenne!" Julianna's singsong voice rose above the music humming from the bookstore's overhead speakers and the faint rustle of other shoppers. "You're here!"

She looked up from the book she was browsing just in time to see a little girl dressed in candy-pink dart around a bestsellers display, pigtails flying. "So is your dad. I suppose it's good that he's here. I hope he has a lot of room on his credit card."

Her words must have carried far enough for Adam to hear. The man strode into the store like a warrior facing a no-win battle. Across the wide chasm of bookshelves and the customer service desk, his smile held enough impact to knock her pulse off its even keel. The man had power. He dominated her senses as he marched closer, making everything else fade into the background.

"Why am I not surprised?" A dark look passed across his chiseled features, but there was no force to it. His brown eyes sparkled with threads of gold and flecks of amber. "I should have known you would be here. It was obvious the girls were up to no good."

"That's me, no good. I'm a terrible influence on them."

"No argument from me. I'm in total agreement." His gaze traveled from her face to the book in her hands. "A romance, really? I didn't peg you for the type."

"Just because I'm not optimistic doesn't mean I haven't ruled out the far distant and probably small possibility completely." She tucked the book in the crook of her arm. She liked the way he laughed. It rumbled low and unexpectedly pleasant.

"Dad, you're *laughing*." Jenny gawked up at him, jaw dropped.

"It's a miracle," Julianna breathed. "I prayed and prayed and it happened."

"It's not that big of a deal." Adam shook his head, scattering locks of his thick, dark hair. A shock tumbled over his forehead, adding a dash of rogue to the mountain of a man in a gray T and jeans. "It's laughter, not a parting of the Red Sea. Go look for your books."

"C'mon, Cheyenne." Jenny took one hand, and Julianna the other. The girls led her to the back of the store. She stumbled to keep up with them, feeling the weight of Adam's gaze as she wove around an end cap and down an aisle of computer books.

"I'll get you a coffee," his molasses-smooth baritone rang behind her. "What do you like?"

"A mocha. What else?" Hadn't he learned enough about her to know the only choice was chocolate? She glanced over her shoulder, caught by the sight of the man standing alone in the aisle, surrounded by books and light and shoppers but still essentially solitary. "And cinnamon flavoring."

"You'll need sustenance if you are going to keep up with those two." He pitched his voice so it rose above the noise without being too loud.

Nice. Cozy. Not that she had time to analyze it because the girls tugged her to a stop in the young adult section. Jenny consulted the list she'd saved in her text messages and the two of them hunkered down to look through the rows.

She should be doing the same, but would her gaze shift from the man to the shelves of books?

No. Her eyes refused to follow the instructions her brain adamantly gave them. *Look away, look away.* Her vision remained glued to the wide back of the man lumbering through the store, tugging at her heart as if a rope bound her to him.

Perhaps it was an aftereffect from being overworked. She'd gotten up before dawn to work with her dad, brothers and Autumn to get as much hay cut as possible. That had to be it. Overwork led to all kinds of problems, which would explain the little hitch in her pulse as Adam stepped into line and she admired his profile. High forehead, straight nose, perfect chin.

"Cheyenne?"

The voice, which came from far away, wasn't strong enough to break her concentration, but the tug on her hand did. Julianna held up a book.

"Is this one your favorite?" Eyebrows arched, forehead furrowed in question.

"Yes." She did her best to concentrate on the letters marching across the front cover. "An all-time fave."

"Okay. How about this one?" She held up another.

"I can't find a lot of these," Jenny said, kneeling to inspect the bottom aisle.

"We may have to order them." She had no

idea how old some of the titles were. "I'll go check in the kids' section."

"I'm coming, too." Julianna bounced alongside her, clutching both paperbacks. "Maybe you should keep Dad company."

"Why, is he lonely? Can't find his way to the coffee counter?" She skirted a display of dinosaur books.

"Yes. Do you like him?"

"He's all right. He seems like a really nice Dad."

"He's real happy these days. Not like when Mom left us. She stopped loving him. Do you think she will stop loving Jenny and me?"

"No, I don't. I'm sure she loves you." Cheyenne set down her book and knelt so she was eye to eye with the girl. She couldn't resist brushing back gossamer-fine tendrils from the girl's face. Tenderness filled her, steady and true. "It's complicated. Some people are never happy even when they have everything that matters."

A shadow fell across her. A boot strode into her peripheral vision, followed by a second one. She didn't need to look up to know who belonged to those feet. She could feel his presence like rain on a southern wind.

"Your mocha." He held two large to-go cups. "How's the book hunting going?"

She admired how his casual, breezy words hid the sadness in his gaze. The man wasn't made only of granite but of strength. She'd misread him. He wasn't unfeeling, but invincible. Unyielding. Steadfast.

"I'm still looking." Julianna took a deep breath, as if to draw away from her sorrow, and turned her attention to the shelves. "I found another one."

"I'm going to steal Cheyenne." A myriad of silent emotions passed across his face, but to her they were transparent. "Will you come sit and have coffee with me?"

"Regardless of the company, I never turn down a mocha." Cheyenne squinted up at him appraisingly.

"Had I known that, I would have skipped the whipped cream," he joked, and she laughed. The soft, melodious trill came naturally to her.

Maybe that's why he liked her so well. She was a ray of sunshine that scattered his shadows. He could hardly feel them as she swirled neatly around a display and headed to the café section, where small round tables were mostly filled with readers, chatters and a serious few tapping away on laptops. He held out a chair for her and caught her faint vanilla scent.

"I have a confession to make." She arranged the little straws he'd poked through the sip hole in the plastic lid. "I didn't go very far out of my way. I was coming to Jackson anyhow."

"It's all becoming clear. I can see why we couldn't go to the smaller bookstore in Sunshine but we absolutely had to drive all the way out here." He folded his frame into the nearly too-small chair and set his cup on the table. Across the store he could just make out the top of Jenny's head; no doubt Julianna was close by. "Are we keeping you from anything?"

"No, although I have an errand with my sisters and my dad in a bit." She shimmered. Maybe it was the light tumbling in through the front window, or simply the way he saw her. "Among other things, the final fitting for the wedding."

"Yes, the wedding. I've heard those are big social events around here." He took a quick sip of coffee. Hot and bracing and sweet, just the way he liked it. "It's all I've heard about from my patients. Everyone's excited about it."

"So are we." She arched one slender brow. "So, you still have patients. I guess that means your reputation hasn't been tarnished yet."

"No one is more astonished than me. Word seems to have spread. A lot of people drive in from all the neighboring small towns."

"I guess folks aren't being too choosy."

"Exactly." He laughed again and it felt great.

"There's no accounting for taste. Those poor desperate folk. Is that what you are thinking?"

"Not even close." Her eyes invited him to say anything. "You like it in Wyoming."

"I'm starting to acclimate." He hedged because he had a life he intended to resume in Manhattan. This was an extended vacation, nothing more. "I thought Cady had lost every shred of common sense when she announced she intended to move here."

"Did you try and talk her out of it?" Interested, she leaned closer.

"Yes." A man could tumble right into her big blue eyes and fall forever. Good thing he was on sturdy ground and holding on tight. No way was there a chance he was falling. "When she told me she'd purchased a country inn, I was stunned. I've known her most of my life and I had no idea that had always been her dream. It must have taken a lot of courage to leave everything she knew behind and to start fresh."

"She's landed on her feet." Cheyenne's smile dazzled. "She's made a huge success with her inn. My dad is sure glad she moved to town."

"I've noticed. Love has always passed Cady by, so I'm glad your dad is interested in her. He strikes me as exactly what she deserves." He took another sip, savoring the rich coffee sliding over his tongue. "Thank you for what you said to Julianna about her mother. My youngest has always been tenderhearted."

"You've done a good job with your girls. Anyone can see you put their welfare first."

"I've tried, but I haven't been what they needed. I failed them." He grimaced from the pain of the truth, the sinking feeling of failure that had been haunting him for days. It was nice to be able to open up to someone he could trust. "I was so busy trying to hold what was left of our lives together, to just get us through, I didn't realize what I wasn't doing for my daughters."

"What would that be?" She tilted her head to one side, concerned and thoughtful, drawing him in with her caring.

"Helping them with their feelings." He didn't expect Cheyenne to understand; her heart had no barriers. "I couldn't deal with mine, so I barreled along, trying to get past all the hardship. But it wasn't simply a matter of time and distance or getting on with life."

"No." She pushed aside her cup and focused only on him. "You were doing the best you could at the time, in what had to be a very difficult situation."

"I should have done better." The truth slayed him. Worse, he wasn't sure if he could do better. He could only try.

"I think you've done all right." Not a hint of judgment, just a steady reassurance radiating from her as if she truly believed it. "All anyone can do is their best. No one is perfect, so you just have to forgive yourself for where you feel you fell short, learn from it if you can and move on. Just keep doing your best."

"That's the secret to your success?" He'd meant to lighten the mood, but humor didn't make an appearance. Instead, the walls he had lowered tumbled down more, leaving him undefended. There was no way to stop the surge of affection he didn't want to feel. Affection, not gratitude. He would be happy with gratitude, he would feel safe with gratitude, but that was not the emotion coming to life within him.

"Trust me, I'm not so successful. Not personally, anyway. I handle everything by denial. It works, but nothing gets resolved." Amused, she shook her head at her shortcomings and took another sip of coffee.

Both girls slunk into sight weighed down with an armload of books. Jenny led the way to the table, where she shifted her armful to show off the titles. "See what we found?"

"Ooh, some good ones." Cheyenne tilted to the side to get a good look and tapped on one of the book spines. "My all-time favorite. I can't believe you haven't read *Black Beauty*. It's so good, maybe I should pull it off my bookshelf at home and read it again."

"Okay. We can read it at the same time." Julianna plopped her half dozen titles on the table, happy with her finds. "See why I really need a phone, Dad? A pink one."

"I don't need reminding." He pulled out some money and handed it to Jenny. "Go get these books paid for so Cheyenne can get on with her day. We've inconvenienced her enough."

"I'm so inconvenienced. Not." Cheyenne gave both girls a hug. It was hard not to adore them. She grabbed her handbag and the romance she'd set on the table. "Let's find the checkout line."

Julianna gathered up her books and Jenny led the way around the tables. Cheyenne couldn't stop the feeling that she was leaving something important behind but when she checked. She had everything she came with—her purse was hanging from her shoulder, her phone was in her pocket and still she couldn't explain the sense of loss as she followed the girls.

It couldn't be because she was leaving Adam behind, she told herself, denying her feelings again. When she glanced over her shoulder, Adam watched her, smiling. She was no longer sure if her denial was strong enough to explain away the sweet pops of sensation fizzing like soda in her stomach.

Adam drained the last swallows of his coffee, standing near the door. He had a perfect view of the girls at the long front counter, Jenny standing on tiptoe to count out the bills while Julianna clung to Cheyenne's side, chattering throughout her transaction. His guard was down, the woman had rendered it useless. Instead of feeling exposed, he felt calm. Relaxed. As if his life were in perfect order when it wasn't. Cheyenne had done this to him, Cheyenne and her cheerful ease and inviting compassion. She had led him unwittingly right where he'd vowed not to be.

I can't be falling for her. The thought should have sent panic zinging through his bloodstream, but it didn't. He tossed the empty cup into a trash cylinder, captured by the way Cheyenne chatted with Julianna and the clerk, bowed her head to scrawl her signature on the electronic screen, tucked her charge card into her designer bag and took the sack with a graceful, sleek movement of her slender hand.

The sun chose that moment to brighten, casting an ethereal haze into the store. The woman had never looked more radiant, as if lit from within. She wore nothing elegant, just a light yellow T advertising a brand of horse feed, denim shorts and sandals, but she was the most beautiful woman he had ever seen, captivating him with such force the entire world vanished. All he saw was her striding toward him, sandwiched between his little girls. His heart fell in one long plummeting swoop he could not stop tumbling without end.

He couldn't let it show. The girls could not know. The last thing he wanted was for anyone, especially Cheyenne, to guess. He squared his shoulders as she approached and hoped his voice came out normal. "All set?"

"I am, but your wallet might never be the same." She put an arm around each girl, who carried two big bags of books. "The upside is your girls will be very horse knowledgeable."

"Just what I was hoping for." His dry tone earned him a smile and her dimples made an appearance.

Breathtaking.

The key was to keep the wobble out of his voice and to hide the hitch in his step as he held the door. She swept past him, unaware of what she'd done. The day was already oven hot and the parking lot radiated heat waves.

The girls skipped ahead, making plans, their chatter as blissful as lark song. He could barely put one foot in front of the other, and he lingered back with Cheyenne. She hesitated in the parking lot, her keys in hand. Sunlight burnished her hair, bringing out highlights of copper and gold. He managed to hit his key fob, the sedan's locks clicked open and the trunk popped.

The scariest thing of all was that he wasn't afraid, and he should have been. He wanted to absorb the music of Cheyenne's laughter and the alto notes of her voice. He wanted to keep her in his sight, to savor the endearing slope of her nose, to memorize the rosebud shape of her lips and to keep falling into her blue eyes.

"Dad, here." Julianna thrust her package at him. He fumbled but didn't drop the bag. He took Jenny's, too, leaving the girls to chat while he deposited their purchases into the trunk. Cheyenne's gaze caught his and she shook her head, rolling her eyes as if to say, "Glad to see you are good for something."

He shrugged, unable to argue with that. When he wanted to be near to her, he kept his distance. He shut the trunk, opened the doors and shaded his eyes with one hand. "Come, girls. Cheyenne has things to do."

"What things?" Jenny asked. "Are you going shopping?"

"Sort of. I'll tell you about it later. Promise."

She backed away across the lot, glancing over her shoulder to check for traffic that wasn't there. The wind rustled and she caught her hair before it fluttered across her face. He wanted to brush those strands away, any excuse to pull her close.

His arms had never felt this empty as he watched her wave goodbye. It was a good thing she was leaving. He needed time away to regroup, figure out how to stop his feelings and reverse them. He did not want to love anyone again.

"Cheyenne is so great." Julianna slid onto the backseat.

"Totally," Jenny agreed as she twisted to watch Cheyenne's truck pull out of the spot directly behind them, one row over.

He dropped behind the wheel, sparing a wave as she rumbled by. Her window whizzed down and her heart-shaped face could not have looked more dear as she winked at him.

"See you all later!" A threat more than a promise, mischief flashing in her dream-blue eyes.

"Bye, Cheyenne!" Jenny hollered out the window.

"Bye!" Julianna chorused.

The truck's horn gave a light toot, the engine purred as she drove away and he felt a *kerplunk* dead center in his chest. Undoubtedly the complete loss of his heart. He buckled up and put the car in gear, not at all sure what he was going to do about that.

Jackson Hole

Reality shifted in place. Dulled by the soda pop bubbles on his face. He recalled, almost just to call an issue, not at all like when he falls from one to another past.

Chapter Eleven

By the time Cheyenne had navigated through downtown Jackson, found parking and squeezed her truck into a spot at the curb, those soda pop bubbles in her stomach were still fizzing. They didn't go away. Hurrying down the sidewalk didn't do it. Forcing her mind from all thoughts of Adam didn't do it. Walking into the jewelry store facing her father didn't do it.

Frustrated, she listened to the shop's door *whoosh* shut behind her, felt the welcome rush of cool air wash over her and managed what she hoped was a smile for the little clan of Grangers staring at her, minus Addy.

"Glad to see you made it, missy." His wide shoulders looked taut enough to use as a crowbar. Poor Dad.

"I wouldn't have missed this for the world."

She wished she could do something to ease his stress.

"I was majorly psyched when the address you texted us was a jewelry store." Autumn practically hopped in place. "I can only think of one reason why we would all be here."

"Me, too," Sierra agreed.

"Me, three," Rori piped in.

"Now, no speculating," Dad commanded in his gentle, booming manner. "We'll wait for Addy. And here she comes."

The littlest Granger girl waltzed into sight, strawberry-blond head bent over her phone screen. She glanced up at the address above the door and back down at her phone. Surprise crossed her face as she yanked open the door, spotted them and broke into an incredible smile.

"Dad! This is a jewelry store. *Jewelry.*" She repeated as if it were the most wonderful word in the world. She launched into his arms. She hugged him tight before bopping away.

"I can see you girls have already figured it out. I told Justin and Tucker this morning." He appeared bashful, blushing a bit, but that only made him more dear, their beloved father. He towered above them as mighty as ever. "I'm gonna ask Cady to marry me and seeing as I'm not the best fish in the sea I want to get her a ring she can't say no to."

"Dad." Cheyenne rolled her eyes as her sister squealed. "I don't think the ring will be the deciding factor."

"Then I'm in big trouble." Dad's dimples flashed. "Will you girls help me out?"

More squeals rose in the air as the group of them gave Dad a hug and dragged him over to the display case where big diamonds winkled invitingly.

"You can see my problem." He shook his head at the dazzle. "Which one do I pick? They all look fine to me."

"Don't worry, we'll help you." Cheyenne wrapped her arm around his. "Can you see how happy we all are?"

"I do. It means the world to me." He blinked hard, uncharacteristically emotional.

"Ooh, look at this one." Addy tapped the glass above an oval gem as big as her thumbnail. "It's very glittery."

"That's really flashy. Maybe something unique like this pink diamond." Rori leaned over the display.

"This marquee cut is rimmed with sapphires." Sierra sidled up close. "Stunning."

"I say an emerald to match her eyes," Autumn

advised as she moved down the display. "Don't think I haven't done a little reconnaissance just in case. Cady and I have been spending a lot of time together, since I've been giving the Stone girls riding lessons over at the inn."

"You questioned her about this?" Dad went pale.

Poor Dad. It must be tough being so big and strong and yet as vulnerable as anyone.

"I didn't question her, no." Autumn grinned mischievously. "We just had a general conversation about jewelry a while back. Her favorite stone is an emerald."

"Choose that," Cheyenne advised her dad. "An emerald encircled by big beautiful diamonds. What do you all think?"

"Perfect." Rori and Sierra chorused.

"Fab," Addy agreed. They all clustered around the emerald display where beautiful rings winked at them, each one lovelier than the next.

Cheyenne's pocket chimed. She realized the fizzes hadn't left and as she fished out her cell they increased. Why did she have the crazy hope it was Adam texting her?

Cheyenne, guess what? Dad got me my own phone and it's pink. Just like yours.

She didn't want to think about why she felt disappointed. As if he would text her. She'd never seen him send a message. Since hearing from Julianna put a smile on her face, she typed out an answer.

Congrats! Glad your dad caved. Now we can text all the time.

Her thumb hit the send button. She caught Dad watching her curiously. "It was Julianna."

His curiosity turned into a smile, no doubt speculation. Well, she was starting to wonder about her feelings for Adam, too. She'd never needed her denial skills this much before. The fizzy pops in her midsection remained, evidence that some things could not be denied away.

"Dad, this is the one." Autumn held up an emerald ring the store clerk had given her. The perfect gem sparkled in the light like a fairy-tale stone. "What do you think?"

Cheyenne felt her father's gaze linger on her for a moment. Their eyes met and she saw his understanding. It was hard to open one's heart again, but he had done it. He had put the scars of his past behind him, gathered his courage and taken the risk. Look how it was turning out for him. Taking the risk had transformed his life, put a sparkle back in his lapis-blue eyes and given him a loving future. Because, really, how could Cady say no to Dad?

You are just panicking, Cheyenne. The realization swept over her like a splash of cold water. All this marriage talk was getting to her. She wasn't ready for serious and neither was Adam, and chances were astronomical that when he was ready, he wouldn't be interested in her. She felt antsy because she *was* getting closer to a man, but the closeness was friendship only.

She didn't have a thing to worry about. Those soda pop fizzes? Forget about them.

"That's the one." Dad chuckled, a mix of happiness and relief and anxiety. "Now comes the tough part. I have to pop the question."

"You will do just fine." Cheyenne squeezed in to get a good look at the chosen ring her future stepmother would wear.

Cheyenne, this. Cheyenne, that. It was all the girls had been able to say all afternoon. Adam shouldered through the screen door to the patio to find the backyard empty. Where had his daughters gone?

"Jenny. Julianna?" He pitched his voice to carry on the persistent Wyoming breezes. Leaves answered with a musical rustle. Birds chirped with a carefree tune. The mother finch in the apple tree winged by, giving him what felt like a dark look as if she hadn't forgotten how close he'd been to her nest with the ladder.

"Jenny!" Worry cut through him. They were as safe as they could be in this town, but big-city anxieties died hard. He put down the book and the glass of tea he'd fetched on the umbrella-shaded table and marched into the yard.

The fence's gate swung open and closed with a lazy creak. At least there was a clue. He followed the trail around to the gravel driveway on the far side of his yard and spotted a familiar dark head and two pigtails hovering in the grass. Concern rushed out of him. "You girls know not to leave the yard."

"But we had to." Julianna popped out of the irrigation ditch. Swamplike water stained her shirt and a wet little something clasped with both hands. Two tiny pointed ears poked up between her fingers and two green eyes blinked. "It's a kitten. I heard her crying and look. She nearly drowned, Daddy."

"We pulled her out before she did. She fell down the bank and couldn't get up on her own." Jenny struggled up the steep incline to stand beside her sister. She checked over the creature with worry. "She could be hurt."

"She needs a doctor." Julianna gently stroked

the striped gray-and-white fur. Tucked in her hands, the helpless animal shivered. "She needs Cheyenne."

"I'll call her." Jenny pulled out her cell, punched a button and waited for the connection. The girls' fears for the kitten were great enough to dim the sun and chase the warmth from the wind.

"Let me take a look." Remembering the boy he'd once been, he knelt in the road. "I'm not an animal doctor, but I know a thing or two."

"She's shaking hard." A frown tugged down Julianna's cupid's mouth. "Maybe she's hurt. Maybe she's dying."

That single sob broke his heart as he squinted at the kitten. "She might just be cold. That irrigation ditch is deep and chilly. You hold her good for me, we don't want her to get scared and run off."

"Cheyenne showed me how." Julianna sniffled, her sympathy for the wee kitten one of the most beautiful things he'd seen in a while. Jenny rushed up, just as dear, just as concerned. "I got her. She's on her way."

"Good." The kitten's pupils looked responsive and even. He stroked the kitten's small nose for a moment before folding back the fragile bottom lip. Both color and capillary refill were good. "We need to dry the kitten off and warm it up. I think it should be okay."

"Thank you, Daddy." Tears stood in Julianna's eyes. "You are almost good enough to be a vet."

"Thanks, sweetheart."

"I'll get a towel. I'll hurry!" Jenny dashed off, dust rising like chalk beneath her sandals as she crossed the private drive and disappeared behind the gate.

"C'mon, let's get this kitten to the house." He rose, glanced down the empty lane and laid a gentle hand on Julianna's back. "You aren't thinking of keeping the cat, are you?"

"Daddy, she might belong to someone. That's the way it was with Clementine the dog, and then Mittens the cat I found after we first moved in. I took them both to the clinic and Cheyenne knew them."

Cheyenne. He could feel the sweep of the wind brushing his soul. The music of birdsong brightened and he felt her approach before he saw her slide around the corner of the gate. His spirit stilled and his lost heart returned to him. Tenderness left him weak when her smile collided with his.

Lord, please. He didn't know where else to turn. *I don't want to feel this way.*

"I see you have a little emergency." She

sailed over, followed by Jenny packing a handful of brand-new towels.

"That was quick." The words stuck in his throat and sounded gruff.

"I was almost to town when I got the call. Perfect timing. What do you have there, Julianna?"

"It's a kitten." The girl held the baby with infinite care. "She was all alone in the ditch."

"So I see." With a gentle movement, she wrapped the creature in a towel, cradling it competently. At the animal's frightened mew, crumpled lines of sympathy crinkled around her tender blue eyes. "It's all right, little one. You are as safe as can be. Just take it easy and relax, Wiggles."

The smart thing to do would be to take a step back. He wasn't prepared for the affection rising up and drowning him. Swept away, he could only stumble after her as she tossed a reassuring grin to him and the girls with the defenseless kitten huddled in her healing hands.

"Wiggles?" He caught up with her, unaware of moving forward or of his feet hitting the soft grass of the backyard. Everything felt surreal and as if he were floating on a wave he could not control.

Vaguely, he realized Julianna clutched his

hand. The girl's lyrical voice came from a great distance. "I knew it! You do know her."

"Sure I do. I gave Wiggles an exam just last week." She crossed the patio and he rushed ahead to open the door for her. "Jenny, could you look in the phone book for the Benton family? Call them for me and let them know we have Cammie's new kitty."

"Okay." The dash of Jenny's footfalls came from far away, too. There was just Cheyenne dominating his senses, her beauty, her kindness, her heart.

Was there no way to stop the emotions pulling him under like a riptide?

"I need an assistant." Cheyenne headed straight to the kitchen table, her focus on his youngest girl, who eagerly leaped forward at the opportunity.

Resist the pull, he thought. Turmoil rolled through him and sweat broke out on the back of his neck from the effort.

"Take a towel and pop it in the microwave for thirty seconds. See if it's warm." Cheyenne's instructions came as sweetly as a mountain brook. Julianna responded, leaping to help.

The emotion became a physical pain twisting like a rupture behind his sternum. He leaned against the wall, wanting to do something to help with the kitten but he didn't trust his legs. How could he stand firm when his knees were knocking?

"I'm not feeling anything to be worried about." Cheyenne's nimble fingers gently examined the kitten's abdomen. The creature mewed again, shivering hard, wet and bedraggled but no longer frightened.

It was the woman's kindness he liked the best. The kindness she'd shown to his daughters, to him and to all living creatures touched him deep.

Helpless, he was caught in the current. His resistance was futile.

"It doesn't seem like anything's wrong." Cheyenne ran her sensitive fingers down each kitten leg. She slid her sunglasses off, perhaps finally realizing she didn't need them indoors. He liked how focused she'd been on her little patient. Her gaze arrowed to his. Did she have any idea how lost he was to her?

"Cheyenne! Here's the towel." Julianna approached the table quietly, her big brown eyes focused on the tiny kitten. Hard not to miss both her caring and her wish.

"You are a great assistant," Cheyenne praised, fingering the towel as if to check the temperature. "I think her biggest problem is being cold. Do you want to wrap that around her?"

"Yes, I'll be very careful. She's tiny." Julianna's pigtails bobbed forward as she cuddled the kitten into the warm and soft towel, safe once again.

A glimpse of the future caught him like a vortex, spinning him forcefully beneath the surface. As if he were drowning, he could not draw in air. The force trapped him in its grasp as images flooded his mind of Cheyenne in this kitchen, her resonate alto warm with love as the girls hurried to set the table, of Cheyenne gazing up at him with true affection poignant on her beautiful face, of happiness filling his soul as his wedding ring sparkled on her finger.

An emotional blow hit him hard and he gasped, as if punched in the solar plexus. He didn't want a future with any woman. He wasn't prepared to jump into a relationship and trust like that again.

"Cheyenne, it's Mrs. Benton. She wants to talk to you." Jenny rushed over with the cordless receiver, so grown-up. He wasn't sure when that had happened, but she was poised as she handed over the phone and gazed up at Cheyenne with obvious regard.

"Great, thanks Jenny. You girls hold Wiggles and keep her comforted." First she helped Julianna settle the precious bundle against her chest before she took the phone. Every little movement she made fascinated him, he couldn't look away as she tucked the receiver against her ear. "Hi, Connie. Yes, I just finished checking her over. Yes, I know how fast they can move, especially this little one."

"Dad." Jenny sidled up next to him. "She's great, isn't she?"

"Yes, she is." The word tore through him, the admission painful enough to make him wince. His throat tightened, affected by the friendly warmth in Cheyenne's tone as she chatted with someone she'd known her entire life.

"That's a good idea, Connie. Wiggles is not too young for a collar and tag." Unaware of her audience, Cheyenne leaned against the counter and he couldn't look away. "Is that so? I wondered when the diner was locked up last week. Eloise and I dropped by for supper and had to go to the drive-in instead. I'm sorry about your job there. Yes, the economy is tough these days."

Jenny's fingers crept into his and held on tight. "Do you know what?"

"What?" he whispered back.

"Cheyenne would make a good mom."

No doubt about that.

"Julianna thinks so, too." Jenny tried to sound casual, as if her heart wasn't already lost.

He understood completely.

"I just wanted you to know in case you like her or something."

"Good to know." He ruffled her hair, the way he used to do when she was just a little one toddling around. He hadn't kept his feelings entirely secret. He'd been more transparent than he'd meant to be.

Jenny launched away from him, leaving him alone at the periphery of the activity. Cheyenne hung up the phone, Jenny joined Julianna at the table to fuss over Wiggles and the kitten closed her eyes, content, purring rustily. The shivering had stopped.

"Connie and her daughter will be right over." Cheyenne sidled up to him, draining the light from the room, dominating his senses, his anchor at sea. She leaned casually against the wall, unaware of his torment over her.

The good news was that at least she hadn't guessed.

"The Bentons don't live very far away." She continued, casual and friendly.

Friendly. That was a clear sign saying, *Go back. Danger ahead.* Why couldn't his heart listen?

"I know Connie from the diner." His voice sounded tinny and distant, not at all like his own.

"Connie's daughter, Cammie, is about Jenny's age," Cheyenne went on breezily, a woman who plainly was not caught in the grip of the same anguish he was suffering. She watched the girls and the kitten with a serene smile. "Have they met?"

The power of speech abandoned him and he shook his head.

"Then this is the perfect opportunity." She blew out a breath of air, sending a shock of red-brown hair wafting out of her eyes. "It's been a long day, and it's not over yet."

"If you are just getting back from Jackson, then you must have had a lot of errands to run in the city." His tongue stumbled but he managed to get the words out.

"Some very important ones for my family. The final dress fitting before wedding, things like that." She kept her gaze on the girls, who did their best to keep the kitten petted and purring. "So much is going on in my family, it's a whirlwind. Justin and Rori are expecting, so that's pretty exciting. Not one of us actually thought anyone would want to marry Justin."

"I've met your brother. He's a good man."

"Sure, but he used to be more than a little gruff. Maybe that's why I have no trouble putting up with you." She couldn't resist a little humor. "I have practice with surly and distant men."

"I deserved that." Humility looked good on him. "I appreciate your effort."

"You should. I've donated a lot of my time to your daughters' causes." It was easier to jest than to say what she really felt. Getting to know Adam and his girls had been her privilege.

"I can see the writing on the wall. One day I'm not going to be able to stop the inevitable from happening."

"Which is?"

"Adding a pet to this family." One corner of his mouth curved into the most stunning grin ever. Dimples cut into his cheeks and manly crinkles etched the corners of his eyes.

A shimmery sensation swept through her, as if those earlier soda pop fizzes had turned into sun-caught glitter. The back of her throat ached at the purity of the emotion.

This had to be friendship, she thought stubbornly. She couldn't let it be anything else.

Chapter Twelve

"Are you sure you can't stay?" Julianna implored. "Please?"

"Please?" Jenny added oomph to her sister's plea.

"I wish." Cheyenne did her best to brace against the force of both girls with their pleading doe eyes. Not an easy thing to do and she failed miserably. "I have to go home and help with the haying. I promised my dad."

"Oh, bummer." Julianna sighed dramatically.

"Double bummer," Jenny concurred. "Are you sure you have to go?"

"I have to help out at home. It's haying season." She didn't want to leave, not at all, and that stunned her. That could not be good. She squared her shoulders, searched through her pockets for her truck keys and headed for the front door.

"It's dinnertime." Adam caught up to her in the living room. "Please stay. I'm grilling turkey burgers."

"Tempting, but time to escape, I mean, head out. The haying."

"Yes, I heard. Are you okay? You're walking really fast."

Pay no attention to his dimples. She fingered through her keys for the right one, although she was nowhere near her truck. She wanted to make a fast escape before she followed her desire to stay. "Just in a hurry. Getting a little cardio in on the way to the truck."

"What you aren't saying is that you didn't have time to stop and help with the kitten." Conversationally, he opened the door, probably unaware that she was having trouble breathing.

"No." The word came out garbled, hardly sounding like a legitimate word. Something seemed to be stuck beneath her rib cage and she couldn't dislodge it. Embarrassing. "I mean, I had time."

"But not enough to stay?" He followed her out onto the tiny porch.

"A storm is moving in." She gripped the porch's handrail for dear life as she staggered down the steps. Amber flecks of light threatened to charm her more thoroughly. *Don't look directly at them, or they will suck you in like the vortex of a black hole and there will be no chance of escape.* "That's life on a ranch. We've got to get hay cut, dried and baled while the sun shines."

"But there's big clouds coming in." Julianna tromped ahead into the gravel driveway, still damp from her journey into the irrigation ditch. "Is the hay going to get all wet?"

"That's why I've got a date with the baler and a peanut butter and jelly sandwich."

"That's my favorite," Julianna spoke up.

"One of mine, too." Cheyenne smiled at the girl, drawing her close for a hug. She couldn't resist the tender wave of emotion filling her to the brim. She held out her free arm and drew Jenny in before releasing them. More tenderness, but she denied that, too. When it came to denial, she reigned supreme. Adam had a dulling effect on her skill, so she would have to step up her game. "I'm so proud of both of you today helping Wiggles. Irrigation ditches are dangerous for kids, but you were very wise and careful."

"Jenny made sure I didn't fall in. She held my hand so I could reach down and get Wiggles."

"We worked together," Jenny said with a touch of maturity.

"Excellent." She had the truck key in hand.

"It was a privilege to see the famed Dr. Granger at work." Adam opened the truck door, his gaze like a lasso to her soul.

She had better find a stronger level of denial because if she didn't, the consequences might be devastating. The trick was not to look directly at him. "Famed, me? Hardly. Notorious, maybe. A bit disreputable."

"More like illustrious." The molasses rumble of his laughter was incredibly hard to resist. She set her chin, gripped her keys tightly and pointed her gaze at the truck's empty seat where she should have been sitting. For some unexplained reason she couldn't take those few steps to climb in. He leaned in so close she could see the beginnings of a five-o'clock shadow on his jaw. "Thanks for coming when my girls called you."

"Hey, they are tops on my list." She wanted that to sound breezy and confident, instead of a desperate response from a woman plotting her escape. If she could just convince her right foot to inch forward, she could hop onto the running board but it was momentarily impossible because her denial skills sapped all her available energy.

"That's something else we have in common." Adam's rugged voice held a note of closeness. If she bridged the scant distance between them, her emotions would tumble in a free fall she would not be able to stop.

Leave while you can, she thought, desperately praying her foot would finally obey her. She wasn't sure if she'd regained control of her voluntary movement or not because Adam chose that moment to move in and wrap his fingers like a band around her arm. Lights danced in front of her eyes and her denial shattered, the only defense she had against him. Her shoe landed on the running board and she plopped onto the leather seat, staring at the steering wheel in confusion.

Nothing felt the same. Not one thing. The sky was still blue, enormous white thunderheads continued to gather at the horizon and Adam's caring gaze hadn't altered as his fingers unwound from her arm. Although he no longer touched her, it felt as if he did. The connection she felt, the closeness of a bond she didn't know how to describe lingered like the last notes of a hymn that would not fade.

What did she do now?

"Will you be putting the hay in bales tomorrow, too?" Julianna asked, up on tiptoe, her wide brown eyes full of an unspoken need Cheyenne tried not to interpret.

"No. I'm on tractor duty early, early in the morning and seeing Cady in the afternoon."

She plugged her key into the ignition but didn't turn it. The alarm chimed since the door was wide-open. "I'll look for you in church in the morning. Wave if you see me."

"Since you couldn't stay for dinner tonight, maybe you could come the day after tomorrow. You know, as a thank-you for helping us with Wiggles." Jenny shared a secret look with her little sister before she edged up on Adam's other side. "We really want to thank you. It's important."

"Oh. Well." Her forehead crinkled as she thought. "As long as it's important, sure."

"I see I'm not the only one who has problems saying no to them." He closed her door, unable to take his gaze from her. The softly slanting light adored her, making her ivory complexion luminous and emphasizing the dainty slope of her nose. "The girls are right, we owe you for coming when we called."

"I'm going to have to start billing you. I don't know what I was thinking."

Her wink and her lighthearted shrug stole him completely. He could fight his feelings, he could try to keep from admitting the truth but it didn't change the inevitable.

"You know where to send the statement," he quipped in return. "Although a word of warning. I may be a credit risk."

"You look like the type." She buckled up, merriment so sweet the hold she had on him cinched up tight. The engine purred to life and she put the truck in gear. "See you all later. You girls text me so I know how you like the horse books."

"We will," Jenny promised as Julianna bounced on her toes, waving. "Bye!"

Goodbye was one word he didn't want to say to Cheyenne. It seemed as if the sun stopped shining and the color faded from the day as she drove away.

"Oh, I just love her." Julianna sighed.

I do, too, he almost said but caught himself in time. There was no fighting his feelings or changing them. They remained like the sky above, fathomless and forever.

"Come, girls, let's go inside." He put an arm around them both, realizing he wasn't the only one staring down the empty driveway already missing Cheyenne. His soul leaned after her, no longer complete.

A knock rapped on her bedroom door before dawn. She startled awake in the middle of dreaming she was racing down the hall late for her final exam, her typical anxiety dream, the one that haunted her whenever she had too much on her mind. She tossed back the covers, the rustle loud in the quiet bedroom. Was it her imagination or had someone knocked on her door?

"Cheyenne? Rise and shine, sweetheart." Dad sounded chipper on the other side of that knock. "You up?"

"Yes." Not that she was prepared to move a muscle, but at least she opened her eyes. Pre-dawn twilight filtered through the curtains. She felt as if she'd been dragged by a horse for three miles as she summoned her strength and climbed out of bed.

Where did her first thoughts go? They rolled right back around to yesterday afternoon when Adam had helped her into the truck. Her head swam at the memory.

Would falling for him really be that big of a disaster? The calm question whispered through her soul as she tugged on a pair of socks and stepped into a pair of jeans. Was there really some part of her that believed having feelings for Adam *wouldn't* be doom? Or was that calm voice a heavenly one?

"I hope not, Lord." She truly appreciated God's guidance but how could her feelings for Adam be a good thing? She yanked on a rumpled T-shirt and grabbed her hoody. Birds began to sing as she opened the door, ready for barn chores, stumbled into the bathroom she shared with Addy and grabbed her toothbrush.

For starters, Adam was only in town for the summer. By the time the school year started, he and his daughters would be back in New York going about their regular lives. She squeezed mint striped toothpaste onto the bristles and started brushing. She stared at her reflection in the mirror, auburn hair tangled, bags under her eyes—she was clearly not at her best. If he saw her now, he would definitely take off for New York sooner rather than later.

"Cheyenne! Breakfast." The door into Addy's room popped open, adorable with her fresh-faced cheer. "Dad's making pancakes. Hurry."

"Coming." She spit into the sink, rinsed out her mouth and dropped her toothbrush in the holder. Addy's footsteps trotted ahead of hers as they followed the aroma of sizzling sausage links, cooking pancakes and fresh coffee.

"There you are." Dad glanced up from the griddle with a spatula in hand. "I was about to eat the whole stack myself."

"Morning, Dad." Addy sailed around the breakfast counter and grabbed the coffee carafe with complete gratitude. "Caffeine. Just what I need. Oh, Mrs. G. remembered to get the coffee creamer I like. She's a total keeper."

"Glad you think so since I just gave her another raise. Can't let that woman get away." Dad gave a pancake a neat flip. "Mornin', Cheyenne. You don't look ready to start this beautiful Sunday morning."

"After a vat of coffee I will be." She stumbled over to the kitchen table and jumped at the face staring in the window at her. A renegade with white-tipped black ears, a long white face and a bovine smile gave the screen on the open window a lick with her broad pink tongue. "Buttercup? Dad, did you let the cows out in the yard again?"

"Yep. Nature's weed eaters. Saves me from having to get out the weed whacker." Dad laughed easily these days. He flipped the last pancake and grabbed an oven mitt. "Don't tear off that screen again, Buttercup."

The heifer stopped in midlick, blinked her long curly lashes and her puppy-dog expression of innocence could have put Julianna to shame.

"So, Dad, any thoughts as to when you're going to ask Cady the big question?" Addy sailed across the floor, two steaming cups in hand. "The wait is killing us."

"I'll do it when I'm good and ready." Dad moved the golden cakes from the griddle to the tall stack on the platter. "You girls don't think she will say no, do you?"

"She would be crazy to." Addy took a noisy slurp from one cup and thrust the other across the table.

"Don't worry about it, Dad." Cheyenne took the cup and breathed in the aroma before taking her first sip. A jiggling sound echoed through the kitchen—Jasmine trying to open the screen door with her teeth. "Cady cares for you the way you care for her. Are you nervous about asking her?"

"Nervous. Nah. I'm not nervous." Dad carried the platter to the table. "It's been a long time since I've been this terrified. Only Autumn getting shot and Tucker trampled by that bronc were worse."

"It will be fine, Dad." She laughed when a moo carried in on the breeze. Two chocolate-brown eyes looked in, watching them all curiously as Buttercup gave the screen another powerful lick. "See, even Buttercup agrees."

"Did she just knock off the screen? What did I tell you, girl?" Dad chuckled as the happy cow caught her prize between her teeth and waved it in the air in victory.

"Not again!" Addy laughed over her cup rim. "Girl, you drop that right now."

Buttercup gave the lightweight metal screen a final wave before abandoning it for the greater fun of sticking her head through the window. She looked around the inside of the house eagerly, her tongue reaching out as if wishing for the chance to grab at all the fascinating stuff.

Dad sighed. "My plan to get rid of the weeds isn't going as well as I thought."

"It never does, Dad," Addy consoled him with a grin.

A faint electronic chime rang from the mudroom. Curious, Jasmine stopped mouthing the door and Lily shouldered close with her teeth clenched around a cushion from one of the porch chairs.

"That sounds like mine." She took a final swallow of coffee, felt the caffeine kick through her system and jogged across the floor. Jasmine blinked, fascinated, and Lily shook her head, waving the cushion like a small square flag. Cheyenne dug her phone out of her purse, glanced at the screen and caught the call before it went to voice mail. "What's up, Nate?"

"Can you make it out to the county highway west of town pronto?" Her boss sounded breathless, like he was running full-out. A door slammed, an engine roared to life and a seat belt warning bell dinged and dinged. "We have a single vehicle wreck. Just got the sheriff's call for help. The truck was towing a horse trailer. It's bad, Cheyenne. Hurry."

"I'm on my way." She tossed her phone in her bag, grabbed the travel mug Addy had transferred her coffee to, waved to her dad and pushed her way out the door. She hated to think of an animal suffering. She prayed whoever had been driving the wrecked truck wasn't suffering, either.

The volunteer firemen were on the scene. Cheyenne couldn't see much with the town's ambulance parked askew on the two-lane highway. The back doors were open and inside Chip Baker, who'd taken an emergency medics course, patched up a bleeding woman.

"You have to sit still, Lisa," Chip soothed.

"How is Ron? I have to see him. We were going to go riding at the state park and watch the sunrise. He just keeled over. It happened so fast." Lisa Parnell and her husband owned the ranch next door. She'd known them her entire life. "Was it a heart attack?"

"They're doing all that can be done for Ron. The county helicopter is on the way."

The helicopter? Cheyenne missed a step. It was a life-or-death situation. When she circled around the ambulance and the fire truck parked behind it, she saw the damage. A truck had rolled into the ditch, dragging a horse trailer with it. Both vehicles were alarmingly crushed.

In the center of the westbound lane lay a motionless Mr. Parnell. Ford, the sheriff, knelt to administer oxygen. Another man crouched with his back to her, giving CPR. She would recognize the thick fall of dark brown hair and mile-wide shoulders anywhere. Adam.

"Cheyenne!" Nate's call stirred her from the horror of the scene. Her boss rose out of the irrigation ditch and clomped up onto the road. "You're a sight for sore eyes. I need a hand."

"Just one? I've got two." She set her medical kit on the edge of the road because she was shaking. So much pain and injury to people she knew rattled her. She drew in a steadying breath, found her professional calm and followed Nate down the embankment. The back of her neck tingled and she wondered if Adam watched her as she climbed out of sight. Nate charged ahead, tromping through the deep wet ditch and onto the grass where the horse trailer lay on its side, the top torn away, a horse sprawled motionless in the field and another inside the broken trailer.

"One was dead on arrival. There was nothing I could do." He raked one hand through his dark hair and the gray predawn light could not hide the grief and failure on his face. "I've got Clark sedated, but he has internal injuries.

I need to get him to the clinic. He needs scans and X-rays."

"Then let's get to work." Cheyenne glanced at the animal in the field, so still, and gave a quick prayer for Ebony. He'd been a nice horse. She ducked to followed Nate into the crumpled trailer where the beautiful bay with cuts and abrasions needed more than a few stitches. She knelt by the gelding's head and stroked his velvet coat. "Hi, boy. Everything is going to be all right."

At least she prayed it would be.

"That's what I told him." Nate had been understating the horse's condition. Sorrow glimmered in his eyes and he knelt to fuss with a splint stabilizing the gelding's cannon. "There's an access road not far from here. I'll fetch my truck and we can winch him into my trailer."

The distant *whop-whop* of helicopter blades grew louder as she checked the IV Nate had started, took Clark's vitals and, alarmed at the low heart rate, prayed. The helicopter's engine whined, so close the deafening beat of the blades stirred the grasses like a wind machine. She prayed for Mr. Parnell and for his wife. As she palpated Clark's belly, she thought of Adam fighting to save Mr. Parnell. What a terribly sad morning.

Nate's rig and trailer came into sight. She

hopped up, eager to get the harness in place, not wanting to waste precious time. The moment her shoes hit the earth, the sun peeked over the eastern horizon. Soft light tumbled onto the scene like heaven's gentle sympathy.

The back of her neck tingled. She spun around, already knowing she would see Adam above her on the road. Silhouetted and backlit by the dawn's mellow light, he looked like the hero he was, a man who fought for life and stood for everything she most valued.

You will not love him, she told herself, but her uncooperative heart refused to listen. Affection lit her up like a country dawn as Adam lifted one hand in a brief wave. His gaze collided with hers and she felt the last of her denial shatter. Someone inside the chopper called his name, but a beat passed before he broke away. Her world changed as he climbed inside; the helicopter lifted off and wheeled out of sight.

Chapter Thirteen

"Look who I found at the back door." Nate's voice echoed in the long cement corridor of the big animal section of the clinic. It was part barn and part hospital with a sterile surgical room down the aisle from the padded recovery suite. This was where Cheyenne gave a groggy Clark a gentle neck pat before peering around the open door.

"Who did you find? Wait, I recognize that skipping gait."

It echoed down the hall with a cheerful rhythm. Easy to recognize. "Julianna."

"It's me!" she sang, sweet as pie.

She knew Adam was near from the tug on the tides of her heart. Weary from a tough morning, she blinked her blurry eyes and zoomed in on the gorgeous man striding closer, flanked by his daughters. His dark gaze held a solemn note of understanding. She didn't need to ask to know he had spent the morning helping with Mr. Parnell's care.

"Surprise. We brought you lunch." He held up several big bags giving off the wonderful greasy scents of burgers and French fries. "For you, too, Nate."

"That's mighty thoughtful of you." Nate managed a wobbly grin of appreciation. "Cheyenne, I'll stay with Clark if you want to take a break. Go on."

"Are you sure?" Her stomach growled loudly, betraying her.

"I've got it covered."

Jenny handed him a cup of cola out of the cardboard carrier and a straw. Julianna gave him a bag of food.

"Thanks a bundle." No man on earth could have looked happier than Nate, who had been going hard since sunup. "Take your time, Cheyenne. I'll call if I need help."

"As long as you agree to take a break when I get back." She gave Clark one last pat. The critically injured horse nickered low in his throat and his eyes drifted shut again.

"Is he going to die?" Julianna's whisper vibrated with seriousness as she peered into the room. "He's got stitches."

"He had surgery this morning. He's real

serious, but he's improving just a smidgeon." Cheyenne wrapped her arm around the child. "Nate is a very good surgeon, so Clark has a fighting chance."

"Good, because his owner loves him."

"You don't even know who his owner is." Jenny sidled up, chin held high, struggling not to let her softer feelings show. And failing.

"He's so beautiful, his owner has to love him. I know I would." Julianna leaned close, a dear weight against Cheyenne's side.

"I know how I would feel if that were Princess." Jenny snuggled in on Cheyenne's other side. "Princess isn't really my horse, she's Cady's, but she feels like she's mine."

"That's why Nate and I worked so hard this morning." With an arm around each girl, she gently turned them away from Clark, who needed healing rest. "Mrs. Parnell loves her horse very much. There is nothing more important than love. It's one reason I do what I do."

"Me, too." Adam's sincerity rang low and rich. He stood ten feet tall in her view, a kindred soul in the truest sense.

I'm in big, big trouble, she thought as the four of them walked side by side toward the door where sunshine beckoned. Every step she made and every breath she took brought her closer to the exorable truth. She had fallen in love with Adam and his daughters. There was no way to stop it. She had passed the point of no return.

Adam held the door. She and the girls sauntered through. Bold sunshine baked them like an oven as they tumbled onto the blacktop.

"We have a picnic all set up." Julianna broke away, pointing toward the shade trees in the grass between the back lot and the river. "The blanket was my idea."

"But the picnic was mine." Jenny trotted ahead so she could smooth down the ripples the wind had made. Rocks held down three of the four corners. "The flowers are from Dad."

"From me?" Adam almost stuttered. "I wasn't the one who picked them."

"Dad, shh!" Jenny shook her head at him as she found a rock to secure the wayward corner. "They're from Dad, Cheyenne."

"Yes, from Dad," Julianna emphasized as she bounded onto the blanket, dropped to her knees and swept up the bundle of handpicked wildflowers. Daisies smiled, buttercups nodded and sunflowers danced on their long stems.

"They are apparently from all of us." He set the food bags in the middle of the blanket. What were his girls up to? Come to think of it, they had been behind a lot of his recent encounters with Cheyenne.

"Thank you. They are lovely." She took the bouquet and admired the blooms. Did she know how lovingly they had been picked? It hadn't occurred to him until this moment when he saw the raw adoration on Julianna's face and the unveiled hope on Jenny's.

"When Nate called Mrs. Parnell to update her on Clark's condition, she said Mr. Parnell was stable in CICU."

"He had a heart attack when he was driving down the highway at fifty-five miles an hour." Considering the other injuries the man sustained in the accident, it was a miracle he was still alive. "God was watching over him."

"I was surprised to see you at the scene this morning." She set the flowers aside on the blanket.

"The sheriff called me and told me to get out of bed and help." He unrolled the crumpled edge of the bag and pulled out Jenny's chicken burger. He handed it over. "So I did."

"You made a huge difference." Her gaze held his, gentle with respect. "After the helicopter left and we got Clark in the trailer, a few of the firemen told us what you did. Mr. Parnell wouldn't have made it without you."

"I was in the right place at the right time,

and it wasn't me." God decided who lived and who didn't. He learned that early on as a resident. "I did my best and I was glad to help."

"You know what this means, right?" She took the burger he offered.

"What?"

"You're one of us now. A true Wild Horse, Wyoming, citizen."

His pulse flatlined as he gazed at her. All he wanted was to get closer to this precious woman when logic told him to run as fast as he could to escape.

"Dad, can I say grace?" Julianna's innocent question penetrated his thoughts. He managed to nod, watching as Cheyenne bowed her head, the tendrils from her ponytail tumbled to hide her face. It took all his willpower to keep from reaching out and brushing them behind her ear. He wanted to trace the smooth ivory line of her jaw and the rosebud curve of her upper lip.

"Dear Father," Julianna's earnest prayer came more purely than the wildflower-scented breeze. "Please watch over all animals everywhere, especially those who are hurt or without a home and have no one to love them. Please answer all our prayers for others. Thank you. Amen."

He realized he hadn't bowed his head as he muttered "Amen," but he figured God would hear him anyway and understand the reason why he couldn't fully close his eyes. He felt his life change in the ordinary moments after Cheyenne's quiet "Amen." The girls unwrapped their burgers, Cheyenne dug into the tub of fries, and all three females chatted while birds sang from the trees.

Places within him long dormant and dark opened up at the music of Cheyenne's laughter. Every missing piece in the puzzle of his life had been found and they all fit into place. *I'm happy,* he realized. Peace filled him with exceptional force, strong enough to wash away the torment of Stacy's betrayal, the bleak years following his divorce and his fear of trusting another woman again. Like heaven's touch to his soul, his spirit found light and she was in the center of that brightness, so incandescently beautiful he could see his future.

His future with her. Afternoons of picnics and laughter, evenings of lighthearted companionship and a singular sense of belonging. Fixing meals, going grocery shopping, having picnics by the river. He saw years of steady love that would never fade. He could trust Cheyenne with his girls and his heart forever. But was that what she wanted? Did he have a chance with her?

"Dad, can we go? Can we?"

He blinked, realizing he hadn't heard the content of the conversation. His daughters peered up at him with expectant hope, excitement oozing out of them as they practically bounced in place.

"I wasn't listening," he admitted.

"Oh, typical man." Cheyenne tossed a fry at him, which sailed past his head. Intentionally, he figured, since she was the most skilled woman he knew. She was probably an expert markswoman. She shook her head, scattering silken strands of burnished cinnamon. "Girls, do you think he heard a single word we said?"

"No," they answered in unison.

"Then I think it should be an automatic yes. That will teach him to listen next time." She winked at him and took a sip from her straw. "There might be a few close calls, but your dad will probably survive. He might be a bit battered and bruised, but he'll heal. Eventually."

"Eventually?" What *had* they been talking about? The chuckle rolled through him. For a day that had started out tough and had gotten tougher, he felt remarkably strengthened instead of drained, whole instead of spent. Life was better with her. He reached for his cup of cola. "Why exactly would I get bruised and battered?"

"The haying is almost done." Cheyenne

tossed him an innocent look. "Which means we will be moving the range livestock to fresh pastures soon. You will be riding with us in the cattle drive."

Fantastic. The lurch of panic streaming into his veins wasn't because of the prospect of getting on a horse. It was because of her.

"Great. Looking forward to it." He unwrapped his chicken burger and took a bite. "Don't look shocked. I'm full of surprises."

"That was mighty thoughtful of the doc and his kids," Nate commented from his desk in the small office across from the recovery room. "Seems to have taken a fancy to you."

"Oh, the girls and I are kindred spirits." Cheyenne propped one shoulder against the doorjamb. "Animal lovers have to stick together."

"You know it." Nate made a notation on Clark's file. "I was talking about Adam. He really likes you."

"Oh." Her face turned instantly hot and tight as a blush rushed across her cheeks and turned her nose as bright as a strawberry. She stared down at the flowers she held in her hand. She had yet to deal with her incredibly strong feelings for Adam. The time spent with him and his girls lingered like a hymn, lifting her up.

"That's what I thought." Nate nodded his approval. "I like the doc. He arrived on scene the same time I did, and his fast action saved Ron Parnell. He's a good man."

"So everyone has said to me today. Right now I'm not looking for a man, good or otherwise." She opened a cabinet door in search of a cup.

"Sometimes we don't have much say in the timing. God does." Nate flipped the file closed. "Why don't you take the rest of the afternoon? You have that thing at Cady's. I'll stay here."

"Are you sure? You've had a long day, too." She felt rosy from the picnic with the Stone family and the following walk along the river. She felt ready to take on any problem. "I have a little time before I have to leave for the spa. Why don't you head home to take a quick nap and come relieve me in an hour? If Clark gets into trouble, I'll call."

"I won't be far away." Literally, since he lived a few blocks over. He pushed to his feet. "That's a good plan. I'm glad to have you on board."

"Glad to be on board." She plunked the flowers into a cup and left them on the counter.

"Any word yet on when Frank is going to pop the question to Cady?"

"Nothing that I can reveal."

"That sounds promising."

Excitement sparkled through her, merry and light. Her life had taken a whole new turn. She waved goodbye to Nate before creeping back into Clark's stall, where the dozing animal opened one eye enough to peer at her through his long dark lashes and nicker low in his throat.

"Poor boy, I'm right here." She stroked his neck, willing all the love and comfort she could into her voice and into her hands.

Seems to have taken a fancy to you. He really likes you. She tried to block Nate's comments and failed. Things were happening too fast, but she'd never felt this way before. In sync, as if they were two halves of a whole.

Did she dare trust in love again? Right now, no words had been spoken, she hadn't committed her heart and if she left things the way they were with Adam, she would never get hurt. She could hide her affections and when he left at summer's end he would be none the wiser and she wouldn't be shattered. She threaded her fingers through Clark's coarse mane, wondering. Is that what she wanted? Would she rather stay safe or did she take the risk?

"What do you think, handsome?"

Clark nickered in one weak rumble, although his eyes remained closed. One ear rotated slightly, as if he were interested to hear more of her dilemma. Did she risk her heart? Was anything worth that risk?

"The thing is, I have this falling-stomach feeling like when you're on the topside of a roller coaster about to go down. It's scary." She kept her tone reassuring. She ran her fingers lightly through his mane. "I don't want to get hurt. It's happened before."

Clark's breathing deepened into a regular rhythm and she dared to hope he would pull through with flying colors. Life was uncertain. It was finite. There was no time to waste any chance for happiness and a family of her own. She loved those girls and she loved their father. Was keeping her heart safe worth the future she might lose with them?

What would the future be like with Adam? She imagined afternoons like today brimming with laughter and funny things the girls said and Adam's solid presence by her side. She imagined happiness and joy so great, she couldn't remember the hurts of her past. She longed for the comfort of Adam's much larger hand in hers. She missed his presence with a physical pain that left her gasping for air. She pulled her phone from her pocket and tapped on the keys.

Had fun with you and your girls today. Looking forward to doing it again.

She hit Send and adrenaline hit her hard. Such a big step to make and her stomach cinched up tight. Her phone chimed. Adam's answer popped onto her screen.

Me, too. The girls are busy planning the dinner they are going to fix for you. It's a big secret. I've been banished from their bedroom. Is there anything I can do for you?

His offer touched her. Her fingers tapped across the keys.

I'm fine now.

How's the horse?

Stable. The next 24 hours will be crucial.

She tried to imagine Adam sitting on his back patio, while the girls played in the room, tapping away on his phone keys. Or was he in the air-conditioned house? She had a sudden insatiable curiosity to know. She missed him, a sign she was already committed, whether or not she wanted to be.

The girls and I said another prayer for him. How are you holding up?

Better than average since I'm spending time with a very handsome guy.

She hit Send and returned to stroking Clark's neck.

You mean the horse?

I'll never tell.

Her fingers flew across the keys.

You're teasing me, aren't you?

His answer marched across the screen.

Someone has to.

She imagined the smile on his face, the dimples creasing his cheeks and the deep, manly roll of his chuckle. A rosy glow filled her, growing stronger every time she thought his name. While she waited for his next text, she grabbed Clark's chart to record his vitals. Adam remained in her thoughts and in her heart, a permanent change.

Cady had been looking forward to a spa afternoon with the Granger girls for a long time. It hadn't been easy to arrange with everyone's busy schedule, but it was good to have them all together. The spa rang with conversations and merriment as she swung by the mini kitchen to sort through the bottles of soda in the fridge. On the other side of the wall, she could hear Rori's conversation with her husband, Justin, Frank's oldest son.

"That sounds wonderful. Thank you, my love." Rori's words were richly layered with devotion and storybook happiness. "I can't wait. See you soon."

Cady entered the private room balancing the tray. Warmth filled her as she looked at the young woman with the golden locks, big blue eyes and a green tint to her complexion. Morning sickness was lingering this afternoon, the poor girl. "How is Justin doing without you?"

"He's hardly missing me. Everyone is pitching in to finish the Parnells' haying. It's almost done. Oh, ginger ale and crackers. Bless you."

"I hope this helps." She set the serving tray on the little table within Rori's reach. "Frank told me he and everyone would be at the Parnells', so I had the cook send over a spread for the hayers and a few casseroles for the family. I feel sad for them."

"They are good neighbors. I've been praying for them."

"As have I." Cady thought of sitting with Frank at church earlier in the day. He'd taken time for the service wearing his work clothes and had herded his sons away with him the moment the last hymn was sung. As busy as he was and worried about his neighbor, he had held her hand with tender assurance during the sermon. He never failed to let her know he cared. "Cheyenne missed the service. Do you think she will make it?"

"I've texted her, but no answer." Rori stirred her feet around in the soaking tub. "She will come if she can. She works hard. I hope she can get a little pampering time in. You are spoiling us, Cady. This is such a treat."

"Trust me, the real treat is having all the Granger girls here with me." She patted Rori's hand before turning away. There were others to check on.

She found Sierra and Autumn in the changing room next door, their voices drifting merrily into the corridor. Cady knocked, although the door was open. Both girls turned, wearing fluffy robes, slippers and relaxed smiles.

"Cady." Autumn raced toward her, arms extended, energetic as always. Her hug was brief but sweet. "This should be fun. I've never had a massage before."

"Me, either." Sierra squeezed in for a hug, too. Such wonderful girls. "After all the running this week for the last-minute wedding stuff and packing to move in with Tucker, this is just what I need."

"That was the idea." Cady hated letting go of either young woman. "I hear Frank is looking after Owen for you this afternoon."

"My son adores his about-to-be grandfather." Sierra shone with happiness, as every engaged woman should do. "Apparently he and Frank are running the tractor."

"That sounds like big excitement for Owen. Frank is in love with that little boy."

"Are you kidding? *Love* is too small of a word. Owen is Dad's first grandson." The dark circles beneath Autumn's eyes testified to the long hours she'd been putting in on the ranch. "Listen to that. Could it be Cheyenne?"

A truck engine rumbled faintly, growing closer. Hope filled her. "I'll go see."

She gave Autumn a hug and love warmed her heart. She pointed the girls to their appropriate massage rooms and headed to reception. A green pickup rolled into sight and parked near the door. What a relief. She had just started to worry about the girl. She knew Cheyenne had been helping Nate with the Parnells' horse.

"This is the best mocha I have ever tasted." Addy swept into the hallway with a cup in hand, adorable with her strawberry-blond hair, blue eyes and Frank's dimples. "You are so totally spoiling us. You know what this means?"

"I'm afraid to ask."

"That we majorly love you now." Addy leaned in to kiss Cady's cheek.

She tried not to let her eyes tear up. Addy had no idea what her breezy comment meant to her. Cady brushed back a lock of hair from the girl's eyes. "Right back at ya. Are you ready for your body wrap?"

"Ooh, it sounds luxurious and relaxing. Do I get to take this in with me?" She took another sip.

"If you want." The Granger girls had won her affections. She'd never been blessed with children of her own, but she couldn't help hoping down deep that one day...

You were going to stay in the moment, remember? She shook herself out of her reverie and opened the front door. A warm breeze blew over her and she savored the fresh scent of Wyoming summer and a hint of roses from the flower garden. Every time she'd let herself hope, the relationship hadn't worked out. The thought of things ending with Frank nearly broke her soul.

"See ya later." Addy shuffled away in her fuzzy slippers. "The body wrap lady is calling me."

"Have fun." She held the door wider as Cheyenne tumbled in.

"Better late than never." Tiredness marred the skin beneath her eyes. "This place is gorgeous and so soothing I feel relaxed already."

"That's the idea, especially after the morning you've had. Come in, let's get you changed. You have been in my prayers, too, all day." Another surge of motherly warmth washed through her as the young woman stepped into her arms for a brief hug. "You look exhausted."

"Clark is stable, that's what matters. He is much better than he was this morning."

"I hear Adam and the girls paid you a visit earlier." She kept her voice low as they walked along the corridor.

"How did you know?"

"Julianna is breaking in her phone by texting me a lot, too."

"Cute."

"I know all about the supper they are making for you tomorrow. You and Adam have been spending a lot of time together."

"With the girls." Cheyenne leaned her head against Cady's shoulder.

So sweet. She steered Cheyenne into the locker room where plush chairs and couches sat in the center of the space and relaxing instrumental music hummed in through speakers. She snagged a plush robe from the closet and slippers from a shelf.

"Cady, can I ask you something?"

"Anything." She laid the items over the arm of the couch.

"How did you know Dad wouldn't break your heart? I mean early on, when he first asked you out?"

"I didn't. It was a risk I had to take." She slipped onto the couch next to the young woman with Frank's eyes. It was a risk she still took and prayed for a happy ending and that Frank wouldn't break her heart. "Love is fragile. It needs constant tending and care, or it withers and fades away. No one knows at the beginning how it will go or how it will end."

"I was afraid you were going to say that." Cheyenne rolled her eyes, a touch of good humor and disappointment.

"I wish it were easier, especially since you

had a heartbreak not long ago." She leaned against the cushions.

"I was in love with Edward, but it turned out he was 'in like' with me. I was convenient. Someone to study with and pass time with. We had a lot in common." Cheyenne's chin firmed, but she couldn't hide the pain. After all this time, she had finally opened up enough to reveal what had happened. "I served a purpose for him. I wasn't special."

"That had to hurt."

"I don't want that to happen again. I got my hopes up. I saw what I wanted to see instead of what was there. I started dreaming up this future that could never be."

"I wrestle with that a lot these days."

"You? Cady, you just don't know how much Dad loves you." She bit her lip. "I want the real thing. True love, a soul mate, not just happily ever after but blissfully ever after."

"Then you have to take the risk. You have to open your heart. That's the only way. When God puts love in your path, you can't be afraid to let it in or you will miss the best life has to give."

"It should be easier."

"I completely agree." They chuckled together, warm and cozy. She could talk with Cheyenne forever, but she hopped to her feet.

"You need to get changed. You have a rose petal whirlpool bath waiting."

"Sounds heavenly." Cheyenne pulled the robe to her. "You would make a good mom."

Tears spilled into Cady's eyes and she had to blink hard to hide them. "That's the nicest thing anyone has said to me in a long time. I'll whip you up an iced mocha with cinnamon syrup."

Dreams she could not let into her heart whispered for entrance, but she stepped out of the room and headed into the hallway. The gentle laughter and chatter of the Granger girls rang through the corridor and followed her into the spa's kitchen, where her cell phone rang. She tugged it out of her pocket. Frank's number lit up the screen, and her whole soul smiled.

Chapter Fourteen

"Dad, stay out of the kitchen." Jenny met him at the archway with a wooden spoon dripping spaghetti sauce in hand. "I mean it. This is important."

"So I see." He glanced down at the iced tea glass he'd drank while paging through his Bible. "I need a refill."

"Julianna will get it." She whipped the glass from his grip and pointed to the living room.

"Is everything going all right, sweetheart?" Steam rolled up from the stove behind her and Julianna stood on a chair, scratching her head as she gazed down at whatever was going on inside the pots.

At least he didn't smell anything burning and the smoke detector hadn't gone off. Things could have been worse. He was unsure about letting Jenny handle dinner, but she had been making mac and cheese and heating spaghetti from a jar for a while now.

"Dad, I'm perfectly capable." She arched one eyebrow. "This is supposed to be a surprise."

"I get it." As he turned on his heel, the faint sound of tires on the gravel turned his attention to the front window. A green truck pulled to a stop and he barreled across the room. His hand grasped the knob, eager for the sight of her.

Cheyenne bopped around the truck, her hair caught back in a French braid, wearing a pretty pale yellow sundress and sandals. He'd seen her herding cattle, riding horses, doctoring pets and shopping with his girls, but he'd never seen her like this. Wow. He gripped the porch rail for support as she bounded up the driveway, the skirt of her dress swirling and his future written in the joy of her smile.

"Howdy. You look lonely." She bounded across the lawn. "Where are the girls? They are usually flanking you."

"They're inside cooking dinner. I hope you are prepared. I'm not sure how it's going to turn out." He managed to let go of the railing, amazed by her. The sun brightened anytime she was near.

"Bring it. I'm not afraid. After Aunt Opal left and before Dad hired Rori and then Mrs.

G., we had an iffy string of housekeepers who weren't good cooks, or in the case of one lady, too tipsy."

"You've survived my barbecuing without complaint."

"Or food poisoning." She glided up the steps.

"You are made of strong stuff."

"You know it." She joined him on the porch and her presence tugged at the worries knotted in his chest, the ones he wasn't sure what to do with.

"Dad! Is it Cheyenne?" Julianna's sandals echoed in the house behind them, her high-pitched voice growing closer. "Is she here?"

"She texted me," Cheyenne confided to him. "I received updates all day long that said things like, 'Dad just dropped us off at Cady's.' 'I helped saddle Dusty.' 'We went riding.'"

"You are being a good sport. I'm rethinking my decision getting her the phone. Is she bothering you?"

"No, she and Jenny are treasures."

Her comment touched him. Words failed him and he wanted to draw her into his arms and hold her close, to cherish her the way she deserved. He wanted to let her know how he felt, but how did she feel about him?

The screen door whipped open and a brown-haired girl tumbled onto the porch, breathless with excitement.

"You're here!" Julianna wrapped her arms around Cheyenne's waist. "I'm so happy to see you. Jenny and me, we've been working hard making—"

"Julianna, you promised!" a big-sisterly voice called out from inside the house. "It's a surprise, remember?"

"Oops." Julianna jumped back and covered her mouth with both hands.

"You are trouble, little girl." Adam tugged lightly on one pigtail.

"I am." She cheerfully seized Cheyenne's hand. "C'mon! Do you know what we should do tomorrow?"

"What's that?" Nearly tugged off her sandals, she stumbled after the child, plunging through the doorway.

"We should go riding. You, me, Jenny and Dad."

"You are full of plans, aren't you?"

"I'm really good with plans. Besides, that way Dad can practice before the cattle drive." Julianna skipped ahead, carefree and confident.

"He's going to need more practice than that." She glanced over her shoulder as the living room flashed by in a blur. She clattered to a halt in the steamy kitchen fragrant with the scents of simmering marinara and cooked noodles. Adam's cautious frown was contemplative, the poor man. She hadn't forgotten his fear of horses. "I hate to break it to you, but you are seriously outnumbered."

"I've noticed. I'm going to have to learn to love horses."

"This way to your table, please." Jenny tapped ahead, leading the way.

The kitchen bore evidence of less-than-experienced cooks. In the sink sat a pot with overcooked noodles stuck to the side of it. Red sauce dotted the stove top in crimson spatters. A few carrot peelings rested on the floor. Both girls beamed expectantly, looking ready to burst as they gestured toward the table tucked in a bay breakfast nook. A lace tablecloth added beauty to an otherwise ordinary round table where a bouquet of home-grown roses stood crookedly in a vase.

There were only two place settings.

"You girls did all this?" She noticed the salad bowls on the table, a foil-covered plate of bread and a small box of chocolates beside one plate. The platter of spaghetti looked as delicious as it smelled. "I'm amazed. What an incredible job."

"It's for you and Dad." Jenny pulled out one chair, gesturing to Cheyenne to come sit.

"Mrs. Plum next door helped us. She made the spaghetti sauce. We just heated it up." Julianna bobbed over to the back door with so much happiness it looked as if she could bounce out of her pink sandals. "It's the same meal from *Lady and the Tramp*."

"Of course. Why am I not surprised?" His amusement rolled like thunder. "Wait, aren't you going to eat with us?"

"Dessert is in the refrigerator." Jenny put her arm around her sister's shoulders and shuffled her onto the patio.

"It's chocolate pudding!" Julianna's announcement trailed through the doorway. "It's real tasty. I sampled it to make sure."

"Good to know." He held Cheyenne's chair for her while she sat. She looked as amused by the girls' gesture as he was. "Where are you two going?"

"To play at Cammie's house," came Jenny's answer as the screen slapped shut, leaving them alone.

"I'm glad those girls are becoming friends." She shook out her napkin. "Cammie is another animal lover."

"I noticed Wiggles was used to being held and spoiled." He unfolded his napkin. "Jenny has a new friend because of you. Once again you have helped improve my daughters' lives."

"Me? I didn't do anything. You give me too much credit."

"Jenny is her old self and Julianna isn't as fragile. She's bouncing around with the confidence she used to have."

"It must be good to see."

"You have helped open up a whole new life for my girls." He didn't hide his admiration. The strength of it wrapped around her with steadfast reassurance and her soul responded. His tenderness, his commitment, his quiet respect for her made her believe. Quiet whispers of fairy-tale endings felt within her reach.

Her hopes for love were soaring and she couldn't hold them back.

"I don't know how or what you did, but you transformed us." Unmistakable affection softened the rugged lines of his face, and he looked at her as if she were the most precious woman ever. "You brought us all back to life."

"It's a little something I learned at vet school," she quipped. Had she ever been this happy? If so, she couldn't remember it. Unbidden images spilled into her mind of a wedding ring sparkling on her hand, of Adam stunning in a tux waiting for her at the altar with love gleaming in his eyes. Endless love. A perfect future. Her future. The dream filled her with longing for what could be and she felt hopeful.

Adam had done that. His quiet, steady kindness had brought her heart back to life, too. Maybe the love blooming between them was strong enough to be the real thing.

I hope it is, Lord. She wiggled her napkin away from the flatware and unfolded it. Across the table Adam sat there, his gaze drinking her in as if seeing her for the first time. Was he feeling this, too? As if borne away on a warm summer wind he could not stop.

"Oh, the girls forgot beverages." He pushed away from the table, his athletic masculine movement made her sigh just a little. "Is iced tea all right?"

"Sounds good to me." She shifted in her chair and something awkward dug into the small of her back. She reached around and withdrew one of Julianna's paperbacks, *Black Beauty*. She couldn't resist holding the beloved book, remembering Julianna's darling texts about her experience of the story. A place was clearly marked in the book with a sheet of paper. She couldn't resist flipping to it as Adam's footsteps echoed in the kitchen as he moved from table to refrigerator.

"The girl has hardly been able to put down that book." Adam's baritone lured her eyes from the page. Everything about him fascinated her. There was so much she didn't know about him, so much he hadn't yet shared with her. "How long does the horse-crazy phase last?"

"I'm not sure, since I'm still in mine." She went to move the paper aside so she could see the page, but her fingers froze. *The Plan* was written in purple glitter ink across the top of the notebook paper.

1. Have Cheyenne stay to eat when she brings Tomasina.
2. Leave Dad alone with Cheyenne at the bookstore.
3. Tell Dad we like Cheyenne.
4. Give her flowers from Dad.

"That's not good news." His voice penetrated her thoughts. Humor drew the dimples more deeply into his lean cheeks. Two glasses clunked onto the table, ice cubes rattling. "Although I already knew the answer. I just wasn't ready to admit it to myself."

Had he known what Julianna was up to? Or had he played blindly along? Iciness slipped into her veins. She'd thought he was falling in love with her. She'd thought their closeness had been spontaneous, as if God's hand were drawing them together. But it had been Julianna and

Jenny. A different and more mature handwriting finished the list, maybe Jenny's script.

5. Candy. Chocolate is best. It's romantic.
6. Make the date as romantic as we can so Dad will marry Cheyenne.

Marry. That one word tore her apart. Hadn't she just imagined Adam marrying her? Hadn't she just begun dreaming of a future that obviously was never meant to be? It had been the girls, solely the girls, they had been behind everything. Not Adam.

Never Adam. She quietly closed the book and set it on the table. Her hands shook so hard she didn't dare pick up the glass of tea. She'd known better. She should have known it was too good to be true.

"I had to hope, but I guess that ship has sailed. I'm ready to accept the girls are going to be horse crazy for a long time to come." He dropped in his chair, his forehead furrowed and his good humor evaporated. "Is something wrong?"

Would he understand why she was upset? He wasn't in love with her. He was simply plodding along, going about his life perhaps not even aware of what his daughters were planning. And if he wasn't aware, then how ridiculous would her broken heart look when he found out?

"What do you have there?" There was nothing more appealing than the concern dark in his gaze. His features radiated a genuine empathy that could not be denied.

"Julianna's book." She did her best to hide her pain as a second wave of anguish hit her. Did she make polite conversation and try to muddle through the meal? Could she endure it?

"She's made good progress." Was that really her voice, thin and strained? She cleared her throat but it didn't help. "I've barely had time to crack open my copy."

"You've been busy saving Clark and helping with the ranch," he commented amicably like a friend, like a man who was not in love with her.

Her mistake. Just like with Edward. She'd made it all over again. She'd gotten her hopes up. She saw what she wanted to see instead of what was really there. She'd mistaken his friendliness for affection. How dense could she be?

"I'm actually looking forward to the cattle drive. It sounds like fun, as long as I get the same horse." He shook out his napkin, the concern never leaving his face. "In fact, I've been thinking about staying. The girls are doing well here. I would hate to mess with that."

"What about you? Your work?"

"When I was in Jackson with Ron Parnell I looked into getting affiliated there. I'm starting to like Wyoming. Very much."

He was staying? Her heartbreak worsened into a physical hurt so overwhelming it was as if her chest wall had ruptured. She dragged in a shallow breath trying to cope, but pain slammed into her like an avalanche taking her under. How could she make it through an entire meal like this? She couldn't hide this level of heartbreak for much longer.

"This dinner has got me thinking." The furrows in his brow deepened, as if he were trying to figure out how to make things right. Clearly he had to sense something was wrong. "We should do this again, but maybe more official. I ask you out, you say yes, we go to a real restaurant."

"Like a date?" She fingered her napkin, focusing on the hemmed edge until her vision cleared. "You and me on a date?"

"I'm sorry. I'm not doing this very well." He squared his shoulders and leaned in close enough for her to see his sincerity. "Would you go out with me?"

Julianna's plan flashed into her mind. Nearly

every meaningful moment she had with him was because the two of them had been thrown together. Everything from the conversation they'd had the evening with Tomasina, to the one in the bookstore, to all those requests for meals and horse rides and get-togethers were the girls' suggestions. Why was he asking her out now?

"You could pick the restaurant. Does that help?" He leaned back in his chair and the gentle question in his eyes asked, please. "I should have done it before. The girls beating me to it doesn't make me look too good. Is that why you are upset?"

"No." She folded her napkin in half, and then in quarters. She couldn't stay here. She couldn't take another single blow to her heart. Clearly, Adam was interested enough to date her. She set the napkin on the edge of the table. Every nuance of happiness died within her. "We have been spending a lot of time together."

"Yes. I would like to spend more." His dimples dug into his cheeks, those dangerous dimples that ought to come with a surgeon general's warning. They pulled at her like a riptide, grabbing hold of her, trying to make her forget the mistake she'd made.

She wanted to say yes, she wanted to believe him. But what then? He hadn't been falling in love with her. No, tonight his interest in her was far more practical. He didn't love her. He was never going to love her. Maybe he just needed a stepmother or a female presence for his daughters.

That's why he was asking her out. That's why he was interested in her.

Agony tore through her, leaving a terrible void in the center of her soul. All this time she had been falling in love with him against her will, and what had he been doing? Passing time with her because she was convenient. Because he looked at her and thought, why not?

"No." There was no other answer, no other choice. He hadn't given her flowers, he hadn't asked her to the bookstore, he hadn't made a single gesture of caring. His daughters had, but not him.

"No?" He winced, as if her rejection could hurt him. That couldn't be the truth. He took a deep breath, as if gathering his courage. "Then maybe after the cattle drive? You said the ranch work was demanding until then."

"I can't. I'm so sorry." She pushed away from the table and scrambled to her feet so blind with hurt she couldn't remember where the door was. "Our friendship ends right here, right now. I cannot do this anymore."

"But I thought—" He didn't finish his sentence. He shook his head, changing his mind. He rose, a man of granite, but his disappointment showed. "Will you tell me why?"

"Next time you decide to ask out a woman, make sure she really matters to you and not just to your daughters." She pushed the book in his direction. Chin up, shoulders straight, she was dignity and strength and independence, a woman walking away from him.

"I don't understand." Her rejection came like a tsunami hitting without mercy, decimating everything in its path. The blow knocked him hard and he couldn't draw in air. "I thought we had something between us."

"I know you do. You are a sincere man, and that's what makes it worse." She slipped away like a leaf in the wind he could not catch. "But I need more than that. I have made this mistake before and I know how it ends. I'm the one who will get hurt, and I don't want to go through that again."

His pager beeped. Mr. Parnell was still in CICU so he had to answer. "Cheyenne, wait." But she was already gone, walking so fast through the house she might as well have been running. Running from him, as if she couldn't escape him fast enough. His knees buckled, he dropped into his chair. His pager beeped a second time. His hopes, his heart, his soul felt ripped away. The future he'd envisioned vanished.

It wasn't until that moment he realized how deeply he loved her. He hung his head in agony as all the light bled from his heart.

Chapter Fifteen

Cheyenne pulled into the garage and sat in the quiet truck, gathering her strength. Tears kept threatening but she'd held them back. The pieces of her heart kept breaking, smaller every time. Adam was a lot to lose, but he had never been hers. Not the way she wanted him. Not the way she wanted love to be.

Anguish tore through her with greater force as she gathered her keys, rescued her handbag from the passenger seat and hopped out into the beautiful summer evening. Dark thunderheads gathered at the horizon but there was still plenty of wide blue sky above. Leaves rustled, grasses whispered and birds hopped about gathering their supper. She settled her bag's leather straps on her shoulder, closed the truck door and crunched through the gravel.

The house with windows open and full of

light beckoned her, but she wanted to be alone.
Grief and loss and disappointment bunched
behind her ribs as she headed up the lane. Buttercup leaned over the fence to moo. Mares
stopped grazing to watch her as she hurried up
the hillside. The wind caught her dress hem,
and the sandals slowed her down. Cool air rode
in on the breeze and she shivered. She needed
to get away. She needed the comfort of her best
friend. She needed to figure out a way to fall
out of love with Adam. He was still in her heart
and she didn't want him there.

She found an extra pair of Autumn's jeans
and riding boots in the tack room and a crumpled T-shirt of Justin's in the dryer. She slipped
into both and found Wildflower at the gate
waiting for her.

"Hi, girl." That was a good friend. She
hadn't even needed to call her. The mare had
sensed her misery and had come. Cheyenne
rubbed the horse's long nose, smiled when
those whiskery lips nibbled at her neck in affection and snapped a nylon lead into Wildflower's halter. She climbed up bareback and
turned them against the wind. Twilight was
hours away, but the light was already thin-
ning. A storm was on the way. *Let it blow,* she
thought, for it couldn't be as decimating as the
emotional one that had leveled her.

I am never going to fall in love again, she vowed. She had expected too much. Storybook endings didn't happen to her. In torment, she gave Wildflower her head and the mare broke into a mad gallop, but it wasn't fast enough to escape the tears when they finally hit.

It was after midnight when Adam unlocked the back door. A single light pooled over the kitchen sink. Emptiness echoed around him. Bless Cady for agreeing to pick up his girls from Cammie's house. Mr. Parnell had had a reaction to his medication and he'd been given a courtesy call to consult. Fortunately Ron Parnell would be on the mend again in no time.

Adam couldn't say the same about his own life. All he knew was that Cheyenne had rejected him and ended their relationship. Or friendship, as she'd called it. He felt hollowed out, as if the grief of losing her had destroyed everything within him. He dropped his keys on the table, where the meal the girls had fixed remained untouched. His stomach growled, but he wasn't hungry. He flipped on the light, looking at the mess. All he could see was Cheyenne walking away from him.

Julianna's book sat on the table. A piece of paper stuck out of the closed pages. He tilted his head to the side and Julianna's precise print spelled out *The Plan.* Cheyenne had looked at the book right before she'd left. A bad feeling settled in his stomach. He plucked the paper from its pages and couldn't believe his eyes as he read what his girls had done.

It all made sense. Their whispered conversations, their numerous attempts to invite Cheyenne to come over and all the texting they did with her. He ran his thumb across the word *marry,* which Jenny had scrawled in her looping script.

Next time you decide to ask out a woman, make sure she really matters to you and not just to your daughters. Cheyenne's comment popped into his thoughts and suddenly all the pieces clicked. He would never forget the pain he read in her eyes. He'd hurt her, and this was why. She thought he was looking for a mother for his girls.

Now it made sense. That was why she said she needed more, that she had the same mistake before. He remembered that student she'd dated in vet school who made her feel convenient and as if she expected too much.

This is my fault, Lord. Anguish carried upward with his prayer. *I hesitated and let this happen.* If he had been man enough to lay his heart on the line, then Cheyenne wouldn't be hurting. In protecting himself, he hadn't protected her. He had made the mistake of holding back. He was reserved. He had always been cautious. That was the problem.

If only he had seen it earlier.

Defeated, he dropped into the closest chair. It was time to hope that it wasn't too late to be honest with her. He grabbed his cell but he didn't want to do this over the phone. It was late; she was probably asleep, over him, never wanting to see him again.

What if she wasn't? She'd been truly hurt when she'd left. So had he. He had to take the chance she was awake. He couldn't let her keep hurting, he couldn't let this wound between them continue to bleed. Not if he could stop it. He had to try.

"This was a bad idea, I can admit it." She drew Wildflower to a stop on the ridge. Rain bounced off the horse's neck and ran in rivulets down Cheyenne's face. Without a hat, the wind-driven torrent pounded straight into her eyes and she blinked, barely able to see.

Wildflower blew out her breath disparagingly and stomped her front hoof.

"I'm with you. I like storms, but this is ridiculous." She should have turned around at the first raindrop but no, she had to keep going. She hadn't wanted to head home and face her sister and her dad because they would take one look at her and immediately see something was wrong. She *so* did not want to talk about this. The humiliation was enough, but the grief was unbearable.

Adam meant more to her than she'd thought.

The enormity of her loss felt insurmountable. How was she going to get past it? What if Adam wound up staying in Wild Horse? She would see him everywhere—at church, on the street, at the store, in the post office. When she hung out with Julianna and Jenny, he would be dropping them off or picking them up. It would be impossible to cut him out of her mind completely. Her usual method of coping was useless. She couldn't deny away the enormous sorrow consuming her.

Wildflower nickered, lifted her head and scented the air. Aware of the sudden tension of the animal's muscles, Cheyenne squinted into the night, instantly alert. Coyotes weren't a danger, and in a storm like this most creatures knew to stay snug in their shelters. Now and then a cougar was spotted in these fields. "What do you see, girl?"

Wildflower stared hard to the north. The dark night and rain made it impossible to see anything but the shadowy outline of the downhill slope and the section road below where rain pounded and grasses blew sideways in the gusting wind. Farther out, shadows milled against the inky darkness. A distant pair of lights rolled around the corner and spotlighted the unmistakable shapes of cows on the county road.

Chances were equal that the animals were Granger or Parnell stock. Either way, she had an obligation to help get those animals back in their field. "Girl, let's go check it out."

Wildflower agreed, bowing her head against the downpour and picking her way along the slope. Rocks rolled and wet clay shifted. Cheyenne clung to the wet horse's back, bracing her weight the best she could to make it easier for the mare. Blinking against the downpour, she breathed in scents of warm animal, wet earth and fresh, clean rain. It really was a beautiful night painted with ghostly beauty and she wished she could enjoy it. Wildflower splashed through the puddles and soggy grasses. Up ahead, a man's figure cut between the vehicle's headlight beams. Whoever he was, the cows responded. Their shadowy figures plodded into the light to surround the man. Their heads went up and their tongues shot out and grabbed at him with great affection.

"Who is that?" she asked Wildflower. Mr. Parnell was still in the hospital, the only Blake son was a marine based in Japan and her brothers would be sound asleep this time of night, since their wake-up call was at four-thirty. Wildflower huffed out a breath. She apparently had no idea about the stranger's identity. The rain beat against the ground in a hundred thousand drops, a symphony of plops and pings as she urged Wildflower up the embankment to the county road.

The sorrow in her heart began to ease. The darkness seemed less bleak as Wildflower plodded onto the pavement, bringing the man and his luxury sedan into sight. Adam. She would know those mile-wide shoulders anywhere and the thunder of his laugh. Shrouded by rain and the night, highlighted by the beams of light, he was larger than life, vibrant and alive and the power of his character shone through. Her heart cried out for him. What was he doing here? Glad the darkness cloaked her, she drew Wildflower to a stop. She had to get her feelings under control before she faced him.

"Hey, that's my watch. Don't eat it. Get back, Shrek." Amusement warmed those familiar notes. "How did Cheyenne do this? Wait, I know. Hey, I have a treat. Come with me."

"Should we go help him, girl?" Wildflower shook her head, perhaps amused. Why did her heart open at the sight of him? Why did her foolish love for him strengthen? Tears bunched behind her eyes as she fought down her feelings.

She could handle this. She could face him like they were distant acquaintances. She could ignore the dreams that had come back to life. All it took was a little courage and she would look him in the eye as if she'd never loved him. Resolved, she pressed her heels to Wildflower's sides. The horse rocked forward and her iron shoes rang loud enough to be heard as they drew closer.

The headlights clearly illuminated Adam calling to the cows as if they were dogs, patting his thigh, walking a few paces and saying he had treats. She shook her head. "That's not going to work."

"Cheyenne." He whipped around, all six-foot-plus of masculine appeal and might. His gaze met hers with pinpoint accuracy through the shadows and made her stomach tumble. Her fractured soul broke a little more.

Be casual, she told herself. *Aloof. Don't let him guess how you feel.* She steeled her spine, rode Wildflower up to the cows and prayed for heaven's help. The weight of his gaze and the force of his interest fell over her like rain. Every step she took nearer to him was like a stake being driven deeper into her soul. "Cows are smarter than that. If they've been fooled once, they won't believe you until you show them the treats. What are you doing here?"

"Looking for you."

"In the rain?"

"A little storm isn't going to stop me." A gust pummeled him, bringing with it the scent of darkness and loss. The heavens opened up, wet fell like a vengeance but it didn't touch him. The sight of her filled him with an unbreakable peace. This was the woman he loved. "I came to find you. I owe you an apology."

"No apology necessary. Come, Shrek. Here, boy." She kept her back to him, riding her horse around the cattle like a cowgirl in a Western roundup. "Come on, you troublemakers, I'll get you grain if you follow me."

The bull's head went up, his gaze brightened and he took off after Cheyenne with a snappy gait. Atop her mare, she rode through the beams, the light casting her in a heavenly glow for one brief perfect moment. Love whispered through him at her incredible beauty that came from so deep. Strong and independent, she rode bareback, just woman and horse, moving in perfect and powerful synchrony. If he hadn't already loved her, he would have fallen right then.

"That's a good boy. Come with me, handsome." She dismounted at the edge of the road and left her mare standing in the shadows. She disappeared down the embankment, Shrek and his herd following in her wake.

Rain fell with deafening force and yet he could hear every brush of her boots in the grass and every breath she drew. He splashed across the empty road. His eyes had adjusted to the dark enough to make out Cheyenne's shadow kneeling in the grass trying to wrestle a post out of a tangle of electric wire. The instant his foot landed on the wet, crumbling slope, she stiffened.

"You don't have to bother. Stay on the road. I can handle this." She might think she sounded breezy, as if she were cool and strong enough to handle anything. She was. But she didn't have to do it alone.

"It's no bother. I want to help." He skidded down the incline of weeds and grass to land at her side. "I didn't know anything about the girls' list. They kept it secret from me."

"It was cute. Really. No harm done." She laid the post against her knee while she untangled the broken wire. The cows moseyed over. Tongues grabbed hold of Cheyenne's shirt and braid. "I've already guessed you had nothing to do with the plan."

"I will talk to them." He sidled up to her and caught hold of the post. The darkness hid the nuances of emotion he longed to read on her beloved face. "You won't have to worry about their matchmaking again."

"Adam, I get it. It's okay." She didn't look up as she wound the broken ends of two wires together with an expert flair. "Let's forget it and move on."

"I can't."

"We were just friends." She gave the wire a final twist, it held in place as she backed away. "That's all there ever was between us."

"*Friends.* You keep saying that word, but you are wrong." He let go of the post. "I never felt friendship for you."

"You aren't listening to me. This hurts too much." The night could not hide the raw pain in her voice as she hiked up the slippery bank. "This ends right here. We can pretend we tied up our loose ends and move on, okay? We can pretend this never happened. I'm good at denial."

"I'm not." He followed her onto the road and swiped a hand across his forehead to rub away the sluicing wetness. "I can't let things end like this between us."

"I know you're lonely. You want a full-time mother for your daughters." Thunder rumbled from a distance and the rain fell harder as if in response. Drops pummeled to the earth and ran down her face like tears. She caught hold of Wildflower's lead. "I know what happened. The girls and I clicked, so you looked at me and thought, why not? They needed a mother, and you and I get along. From your perspective, I must look pretty safe. I get that."

"Safe?" He could have been a mountain, solitary in the rain. Remote granite without a single speck of emotion at all. "That makes me sounds like a terrible man. Is that what you think of me?"

"You didn't mean it maliciously. I know that about you." She was tearing apart. Nothing had hurt so much, not one thing. "I don't want to be someone you settle for or anyone settles for. I don't want to mean so little."

She wanted to harden her heart against him, but she loved him still. The bond between his soul and hers remained; maybe it had been there all along, the reason why she could sense the deepest layers of his emotions and why she could see the sorrow gathering within him. Could he feel her shattered heart? "This is hurting me, and I need it to stop."

"I do, too." He closed the distance between them, towering above her as dark as the storm. He caught a rivulet of rain trailing down her cheek, his skin warm, his touch comforting. "I should have said this when I first realized how I felt. I spent a lot of precious time afraid to open up. I didn't realize I was hurting you or that it would drive us apart. I'm not just passing time with you. I'm not settling."

"You are doing this for your girls." She had to stay firm. She could not believe in what did not exist. She had to be strong and protect her heart.

"I am doing this for you. I am standing in the rain in the wee hours of the morning with mud on my shoes and cow spittle on my shirt because I couldn't even try to sleep thinking about how you were hurting. I am responsible for that and I am so, so sorry." Iron rang in his words, solid and believable, an unquestionable truth. "You should know you are not a safe woman. Not to me. You are the most inconvenient, unsafe, dangerous female I have ever come across."

"Me? You are making that up."

"I'm not that imaginative." Couldn't she see what she meant to him? How incredible she was? Didn't she have the slightest idea what she'd done to him? "You've turned my world upside down and me inside out. You make it difficult to breathe, impossible to think and my common sense flew out the window the moment I laid eyes on you. My life, my girls, me, it's all changed. It is never going to be the same. You did that."

"No, it was God, it was you, it was Wyoming."

"It was you." Tenderness filled him, heavenly, infinite tenderness. It was her that mattered, bright, beautiful amazing Cheyenne. "Losing you is like the sun going out forever, the worst darkness I can endure."

He had failed to be what she needed. He would never do that again. He would endure anything to take her pain away, so he bared his soul.

"I fell in love with you the moment you climbed out of your green pickup and saved my car from Shrek." He watched her expression change from denial to disbelief. "I didn't want to. I fought it, I ignored it, I refused to act on it, but that doesn't change the truth."

"You don't love me." Back to denial, she shook her head, as if she knew his heart better than he did.

"I loved you then. I love you more now. I will love you even more tomorrow. You still don't believe me, do you?"

"I can't." Why was he doing this to her? Saying everything she wanted to hear, the words that mattered most. She'd given up on love. She was no princess, just an ordinary girl. Men did not fall at her feet and promise to devote themselves to her forever. She had learned her lesson. She was not going to believe again.

"You are the light in my world. I am forever devoted to you. I don't want to live without you. Thank God He brought you into my life." He lowered onto one knee, on the desolate country road in the middle of a puddle. In the faint glow of the headlights, he looked like a knight of old with his invincible shoulders and stalwart heart. "Marry me, Cheyenne. Say yes, and I vow I will spend each and every day of our lives showing you the depth of my devotion and love for you."

"You're proposing?"

"Be my wife because we are a perfect match. Because you are my sweetheart, the missing half of my soul. You are the most special woman I have ever known and I want to give you the fairy tale."

"The fairy tale?" Oh, he made her want to believe.

"You know the stories. The beautiful princess, the prince, the romance, the wedding. The happily ever after." He gazed up at her with his entire soul revealed. What she read there made her throat ache. Tears burned behind her eyes.

He gathered her hands in his with care. The solid, soothing contact hooked her spirit and captured her soul. His baritone rang richly with the immeasurable love in his heart. "Happy doesn't sound good enough for you, but joyfully ever after doesn't sound quite right."

"Blissfully ever after."

"That's right." He stood, rising to his towering height, holding her hands. Promises of forever shone in his eyes as dark as the night as he slanted his mouth over hers. His kiss was flawless, everything a kiss should be. Proof that his love for her was real. The purity of his tenderness whispered in her soul and she could see forever. Her dreams returned, brighter than before. She saw images of a spring wedding with family and friends, Jenny as a bridesmaid and Julianna as a flower girl. Flashes of their life together riding horses, going on picnics, watching the birds in the backyard. There would be a baby one day and the dog she'd always been meaning to get to complete their happy family, their blissful life. She believed. She finally believed. The power of his honest feelings convinced her.

"Yes, I will marry you," she whispered against his kiss. "I love you, Adam."

"Not as much as I love you."

The rain ceased, the winds stilled and Shrek mooed scoldingly.

"I won't forget to get your grain," she told the bull. She and Adam laughed together as moonlight broke through the clouds to shine on them like heaven's grace.

Cheyenne (Final)

Epilogue

"Cady, don't leave us."

Cady froze midstep in the echoing church foyer. The ceremony had gone off without a hitch, Sierra and Tucker were officially married and no one looked prettier in her traveling clothes than Sierra. Luminous with joy, she fussed with her diamond necklace, a beautiful family heirloom Frank had given her. Cady glanced around at the faces of the Granger girls, alarmed at the idea of her leaving them alone. "I love that I'm wanted here, but this is clearly a sister moment. I don't want to intrude."

"Impossible." Cheyenne marched over in a light blue bridesmaid's dress and took her firmly by the hand. "You have to stay, but it might be a teary moment. Brace yourself."

"It's totally getting sappy," Addy warned with a wink as she held out a slim gold chain.

"Sierra, you are officially one of us now, so you get what I'm going to start calling a Granger girls bracelet, thank you to Cady for the term. We celebrate every good change in our lives with a charm. See, there's one for Rori joining our family, one for Autumn's wedding. Now there is one for yours."

"Oh, it's beautiful." Sierra fingered the gold charm in the shape of a little family. "Our wedding date is engraved on the back."

"It's an important date," Rori explained.

"The day you became our sister." Autumn held out her arms. "Group hug."

"I told you," Addy whispered as her arm settled around Cady's shoulders. "Sappy."

"Sappy, but nice." She was touched the girls would include her. So thoughtful. She loved them so much. The group hug was cheerful and sweet and over too soon. The girls broke into chatter over last-minute things—Cheyenne had agreed to take care of Owen's dog, Puddles, Addy would pick up Sierra's mail and Autumn would keep an eye on the construction crew renovating Tucker's house.

Not wanting to intrude, she opened the church door and peeked out. A crowd had gathered on the front lawn, friends, family and neighbors chatting and laughing. She adored being a part of this small-town community and there were so many people she wanted to spend time talking with. Martha Wisener caught her eye and waved. She waved back and kept scanning the crowd. It was her heart she followed, which took her straight to Frank.

She was hardly aware of tapping down the steps. When his gaze met hers across the church's crowded front lawn, it was like being touched by grace.

She felt young, timeless, full of hope. The power of love made her see nothing and no one save for him. He tipped his Stetson respectfully, his gaze never leaving hers. He might be talking with the mayor and Chip Baker, but she felt his attention rivet to her like a charge. Something incredible bound them together, beyond words or measure.

I love this man way too much, she thought, weaving through the crowd as Frank, so dashing in his tux, broke away from his friends. Every step he took toward her stole the oxygen from the atmosphere. She felt light-headed and a little dizzy, overwhelmed with emotion.

"How are the girls?" He took her hand in his and her dizziness vanished. Her soul stilled when he gazed into her eyes.

"Fine. Sierra is about ready to throw the bouquet."

"I've been waiting for this moment a long

time." His hand settled lightly on the small of her back, guiding her toward the church.

"Because you never thought Tucker would settle down?"

"I worried about that boy, but he's turned out just fine. He and Sierra will be good together." He pulled her gently along. Was it her imagination or was he trembling just a bit? That was not like him at all.

"Are you holding up, all right?" she asked, concerned. Frank was close to all his children, so having yet another child get married must be affecting.

"Sure, I'm fine. Just stand right about here front and center." He nudged her a few inches over so they were staring at the front steps. "Here they come."

Impossible not to hear his affection and pride. She looked up as Sierra and Tucker filed out of the doorway, ready to leave for their flight. Owen clung to his new father's hand, excited about their trip to Hawaii. They stood together, the happiest family in existence. Cheers went up from the hometown crowd and Sierra's new bracelet sparkled as she gripped her bouquet.

"Are you ready, single ladies?" she called out, and the crowd answered with more shouts and cheers.

"I have a good feeling about this bouquet." She waved the flowers high, as if to give heaven a good look. "Rori caught the bouquet at our good friend Terri's wedding. Autumn caught the bouquet at Rori's wedding. I caught the bouquet at Autumn's wedding and you can all see how well that worked out for me. Are you seeing a trend here?"

"Throw it to me!" Ivy Tipple called out. "I wouldn't mind being married next."

"Or me!" joked Arlene Miller, making the audience laugh.

Cady laughed, too. Everyone was happy on this glorious day.

"I predict whoever catches this bouquet will follow in my footsteps soon." Sierra turned a few inches to face the crowd.

To face her. It looked like the girl was going to throw right down the center. She imagined all the single ladies in town crowding over to try to be the next bride. Instead of throwing long, Sierra gave her flowers a small toss, the bundle of white and pink roses sailed through the air and directly into Cady's hands.

"Way to go, Cady!" Martha Wisener hooted from the sidelines.

Shock washed over her. Oohs and aahs rose from the bystanders as Frank leaned in close.

"Good catch," he said in a low baritone filled with promise.

"It just tumbled into my hands. I didn't try to catch it." She blushed, befuddled. "Sierra threw it straight to me."

"That's because I asked her to." Frank's kiss brushed her cheek. "There seems to be something tied to the ribbon. Let's see what it is."

He was right. Something glittered there in a flash of gold, a sparkle of white and a glimmer of flawless green. She watched as he untied an exquisite, expensive and stunning emerald ring from the bouquet's blue ribbon.

Tears slipped into her eyes, blurring the world into smudges as Frank bent down on one knee. Her heart stopped. Her knees buckled. Happiness spilled over as tears ran down her cheeks. She realized the Granger family had gathered in a loving circle. Rori hand in hand with Justin. Autumn with her head resting on Ford's shoulder. Cheyenne and Addy arm in arm. Tucker, Sierra and Owen on the steps. Frank took her left hand in his. Such strong but gentle hands.

"Cady Leigh Winslow, will you be my wife?" His question rang with the kind of love a woman dreamed about all her life. He was her everything, her greatest wish come true.

"Yes, Frank. I would love to marry you."

Cheers rang out from the crowd but it was the reaction of the people in the circle surrounding her that mattered most as Frank slipped the ring on her finger. Autumn and Sierra rushed up to hug her, Rori cried, Cheyenne kissed her cheek and Addy cheered. Justin and Tucker shook her hand.

She was going to be Frank's wife. Heavenly joy washed over her as he folded her tenderly in his powerful arms. She leaned her cheek against his wide, dependable chest, home at last.

Cheyenne swiped the tears from her eyes, gave Sierra a hug and wished her safe travels. Tucker looked happy as he escorted his wife and son down the walkway as rose petals rained down upon them.

"Did Frank think up that proposal all by himself?" Adam asked as he took her hand. How wonderful it felt as his fingers twined through hers, a perfect fit.

"He did, although he told us what he was going to do. My dad is a romantic at heart. Who knew?" She went up on tiptoe to peer through the crowd. Dad kept Cady close, his arm was around her waist, and the happiest grin in the world shone on his face. "He really loves Cady. What they have is the real thing. True love. A fairy-tale ending."

"So do we."

"Yes, we do." She believed, she truly did. She was living the story. Her handsome prince looked incredible in a tux with the wind tousling his dark hair. His smile moved through her like joy, and the link of their hearts reached all the way to their souls.

Now that neither of them were fighting their feelings, they could concentrate on the romance. What a romance. Adam had surprised her with roses at her office, which he vowed to do every week as long as he lived to show his devotion. He had bought three horses from Cady, two for his girls and one for him. He and Hershey were getting to know one another and tomorrow afternoon she would give Adam his first riding lesson. His focused and loving attention had been steady and quiet and true. He was a man she could believe in for all time.

"Our wedding might be the next one in this town." He drew her closer.

"That depends on when Dad and Cady set their date." She beamed up at him, the precious love he read in her blue eyes made emotion gather in his throat.

Thank You, Father, for leading me here. He had found the man he used to be. And as for his dreams, he had been blessed with better ones than he had ever imagined. He brushed a tendril of auburn hair away from her face, just to touch her. Tenderness rolled through him like an ocean wave that had no end. She was a rare and precious gift he would spend the rest of his life honoring.

"I'm guessing by the look of things, Dad and Cady's wedding might be sooner rather than later." Cheyenne gestured toward the happy couple surrounded by Martha Wisener, Arlene Miller and Sandi Walters, who were admiring Cady's ring. "My guess is that I might have a new stepmother before the year ends."

"I think you are right." His gaze darkened as he leaned in for a kiss. Not even a fairy-tale kiss could be as romantic or as pure as the respectful brush of his lips to hers. So infinitely tender and exquisitely gentle, it felt as if their souls brushed.

She smiled up at him, he was her true anchor, her deepest wish come true.

"Cheyenne! Cheyenne!" Julianna's high voice rose above the buzz of the crowd. She skidded to a stop, her purple dress swishing around her knees. "Come quick! Jenny's with Lady."

"Who's Lady?" She asked the question, but she already knew. Lady was an animal in need.

"Cammie's friend said someone threw her

out of a car and drove off. She's having puppies." Worry crinkled her darling button face. "We have to help her."

"Yes, we do." Cheyenne loved her life, she loved her job and she was going to love being a stepmom and wife. Joy lifted her up as Adam's hand tightened around her own, his silent offer of help as he came along, too. No, joy was too small of a word for what she felt. This was bliss.

Her blissfully ever after.

* * * * *

Dear Reader,

Welcome back to Wild Horse, Wyoming. I hope you have been enjoying the Granger Family Ranch stories as much I'm loving writing them. I have been especially looking forward to telling Cheyenne's story. Maybe because she's a vet and, being the animal lover that I am, I couldn't wait to fill these pages with animal characters. But more important because I fell in love with little Julianna and Jenny in Eloise's book, and I was excited to write about their efforts to match Cheyenne up with their dad. Cheyenne is recovering from a broken heart. Adam is disenchanted with marriage due to an unfaithful wife who abandoned him and his girls. What are the chances these two hearts can love again, and will God give them the opportunity to find out?

I hope you have fun revisiting the Granger family, who have become very close to my heart. Thank you for journeying to Wild Horse, Wyoming, with me.

As always, wishing you love and peace,

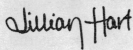

Questions for Discussion

1. What are your first impressions of Cheyenne? How would you describe her? What do you think she is looking for in life?

2. What are your first impressions of Adam? How does he react to seeing Cheyenne? What does this tell you about his character? How do you know he's a good man? How has his wife's abandonment affected him?

3. What do you think of Jenny and Julianna? What role do they play in the story? What do you like most about each girl?

4. What kind of father do you think Adam is? What does it say about him that he moved his girls to Wyoming for the summer? That he wants them to be close to Cady?

5. How does knowing Adam affect Cheyenne? How does knowing Cheyenne change Adam?

6. When does Adam begin to feel he can trust Cheyenne enough to open up? Why is this significant for him?

7. How did Cheyenne's last relationship end, and how did it hurt her? How does this influence what she expects from Adam? What do you admire about her character?

8. What are Adam's strengths as a character? What are his weaknesses? What do you come to admire about him?

9. What values do you think are important in this book?

10. When did you realize that Julianna and Jenny were playing matchmakers? What impact does this have on the story? On Cheyenne and Adam's relationship?

11. What do you think are the central themes in this book? How do they develop? What meanings do you find in them?

12. When does Cheyenne realize she's in love with Adam? When does Adam realize he's in love with Cheyenne?

13. How does God guide both of them? How is this evident? How does God gently and quietly lead them to true love?

14. What role do the animals play in the story?

15. There are many different kinds of love in this book. What are they? What do Cheyenne and Adam learn about true love?

LARGER-PRINT BOOKS!

GET 2 FREE
LARGER-PRINT NOVELS
PLUS 2 FREE
MYSTERY GIFTS

Love Inspired

Larger-print novels are now available...

YES! Please send me 2 FREE LARGER-PRINT Love Inspired® novels and my 2 FREE mystery gifts (gifts are worth about $10). After receiving them, if I don't wish to receive any more books, I can return the shipping statement marked "cancel". If I don't cancel, I will receive 6 brand-new novels every month and be billed just $4.99 per book in the U.S. or $5.49 per book in Canada. That's a saving of at least 23% off the cover price. It's quite a bargain! Shipping and handling is just 50¢ per book in the U.S. and 75¢ per book in Canada.* I understand that accepting the 2 free books and gifts places me under no obligation to buy anything. I can always return a shipment and cancel at any time. Even if I never buy another book, the two free books and gifts are mine to keep forever.

122/322 IDN FEG3

Name	(PLEASE PRINT)
Address	Apt. #
City	State/Prov.	Zip/Postal Code

Signature (if under 18, a parent or guardian must sign)

Mail to the **Reader Service**:
IN U.S.A.: P.O. Box 1867, Buffalo, NY 14240-1867
IN CANADA: P.O. Box 609, Fort Erie, Ontario L2A 5X3

Not valid to current subscribers to Love Inspired Larger-Print books.

**Are you a current subscriber to Love Inspired books
and want to receive the larger-print edition?
Call 1-800-873-8635 or visit www.ReaderService.com.**

* Terms and prices subject to change without notice. Prices do not include applicable taxes. Sales tax applicable in N.Y. Canadian residents will be charged applicable taxes. Offer not valid in Quebec. This offer is limited to one order per household. All orders subject to credit approval. Credit or debit balances in a customer's account(s) may be offset by any other outstanding balance owed by or to the customer. Please allow 4 to 6 weeks for delivery. Offer available while quantities last.

Your Privacy—The Reader Service is committed to protecting your privacy. Our Privacy Policy is available online at www.ReaderService.com or upon request from the Reader Service.

We make a portion of our mailing list available to reputable third parties that offer products we believe may interest you. If you prefer that we not exchange your name with third parties, or if you wish to clarify or modify your communication preferences, please visit us at www.ReaderService.com/consumerschoice or write to us at Reader Service Preference Service, P.O. Box 9062, Buffalo, NY 14269. Include your complete name and address.

LILP11B

Love Inspired®
SUSPENSE
RIVETING INSPIRATIONAL ROMANCE

Watch for our series of edge-
of-your-seat suspense novels.
These contemporary tales
of intrigue and romance
feature Christian characters
facing challenges to their faith...
and their lives!

AVAILABLE IN REGULAR
& LARGER-PRINT FORMATS

For exciting stories that reflect traditional values,
visit:
www.ReaderService.com

LISUSDIR11B

ReaderService.com

You can now manage your account online!

- Review your order history
- Manage your payments
- Update your address

We've redesigned the Reader Service website just for you.

Now you can:

- Read excerpts
- Respond to mailings and special monthly offers
- Learn about new series available to you

Visit us today:

www.ReaderService.com

RS10

anything but the shadowy outline of the distant
hill slope and the section road below, where